Praise for Julia's Gifts

"Graced with soulful sonnets and life-and-death situations, this is no simple romance. It's a strong and tender Catholic historical novel about growing in maturity and fortitude while discovering the power of hope, self-sacrifice, and prayer. I read Julia's Gifts within two days, but this touching story of faith and devotion is sure to leave a lasting impression!"
Therese Heckenkamp, *award-winning author*

"Award-winning author Ellen Gable has created a stunning love story set amidst the backdrop of World War I. Filled with adventure, romance, and intrigue, this gripping tale will keep you on the edge of your seat. There is so much to treasure in this beautifully-written book: miracles of faith, the power of prayer, the strength of true love, and the grace in using one's God-given gifts to overcome seemingly insurmountable obstacles make this an outstanding and unforgettable book." Jean M. Heimann, author, *Fatima: The Apparition That Changed the World*

"A sweet romance set amidst the carnage of World War I France, Julia's Gifts is filled with fascinating historical detail and a reminder that love never fails and that miracles – great and small – happen all around us."
Carolyn Astfalk, author, *Stay With Me*

"Julia's Gifts is a sweet and touching love story laced with beautiful messages. Well-researched, the dialog and details make the story feel genuine, taking readers back to the WWI era. Following Julia as she works overseas as a volunteer medical aide opened my eyes to the hardships of war and especially the great trials and sacrifices of the nurses and volunteers. This story touched my heart in many ways, but the poems written by the character Major Peter Winslow are simply amazing." Theresa Linden, author of award-winning Catholic teen fiction

"The descriptions of war-torn France felt very authentic and really helped me to envision actual environment. Julia's dreams for her future husband face unexpected and ingenious twists and turns. Julia's Gifts is a romantic drama that unfolds far from home—but takes us to the heart of home along the way."
A.K. Frailey, author, *Last of Her Kind*

Julia's Gifts
(Great War Great Love
Book One)

A Novel

By Ellen Gable

God bless you!

Ellen Gable Hrkach

Full Quiver Publishing
Pakenham, Ontario

Julia's Gifts
(Great War Great Love
Book One)
Copyright 2017 Ellen Gable

Published by
Full Quiver Publishing
PO Box 244
Pakenham, Ontario K0A 2X0
www.fullquiverpublishing.com

ISBN Number: 978-0-9879153-0-6

Printed and bound in the USA

Cover design: James Hrkach, Ellen Hrkach

Background cover photo:

Phinou (Wikimedia Commons)

The Glade; The Paladin Unmade;
No Light of Stars No Moon; On Wings of Love
and *Still Lost If Not For Stars*
sonnets copyright 2017 James Hrkach
used with permission

NATIONAL LIBRARY OF CANADA

CATALOGUING IN PUBLICATION

Published by FQ Publishing

A Division of Innate Productions

Dedicated to the memory of
Aunt Flossie (1917-1988),
who was born during the Great War
and was like a second mother to me

O Mary, Conceived Without Sin,
Pray For Us Who Have Recourse To Thee

"Continue always to pray the Rosary every day. The war is going to end, and the soldiers will soon return to their homes."
Our Lady of Fatima, October 13, 1917

"The true soldier fights not because he hates what is in front of him, but because he loves what is behind him."
G. K. Chesterton

"O outstanding miracle! O marvelous and most divine Sacrament! Common bread is lifted up from the altar; the immortal Flesh of Christ is set down upon it. What was natural food has become spiritual food. What was the momentary refreshment of man has been made the eternal and unfailing nourishment of angels."
Stephen, Bishop of Autun (1139)

Chapter 1
My Beloved

December 17, 1917

The bustling streets of Center City Philadelphia shimmered with electric lights, heralding that Christmas was near. Julia Marie Murphy lifted her head and gazed upward. The night sky was filled with snow clouds, the air brisk. She pulled on her gloves and buttoned the top of her coat. Her thoughts turned to her future husband. *Dear God in heaven, please protect my beloved.*

Tens of thousands of American men had already enlisted to fight in this "Great War." The gentlemen that Julia knew seemed anxious to join, and Julia thanked God that her three brothers were too young to fight.

In a few short weeks, it would be 1918. All of her father's friends and acquaintances expected the war to end soon, hopefully before the middle of the year. But 1918 held far more significance for Julia. This would be the year that she would turn 21.

She approached Lit Brothers department store, admiring the display windows that were outlined with colored electric lights. Julia was thankful that it was Monday. If it were Thursday, the ban on electric lights (in support of the war effort) would mean the windows would be dark.

Julia stared, transfixed, through the window at the tall display. Shimmery red fabric hung from a back wall, a beautiful sterling silver pocket watch lay on top of a cylindrical pedestal. Her eyes widened when she saw the price tag: $12.25, almost 20 percent of her annual salary. But it *was* beautiful and every man needed one. The price notwithstanding, this would be a perfect gift for her beloved. Yes, it was extravagant, especially during wartime. Yes, there were less expensive items she could purchase. It didn't matter. *This* was the ideal gift.

After purchasing it, she took it to the engraving department on the second floor. Behind the counter, the tall, lanky middle-aged man with a handlebar mustache smiled. "What would you like engraved on this?"

"To my beloved, next line, all my love, Julia."

His eyebrows lifted. "I'm certain the gentleman would prefer to have his Christian name engraved on this lovely timepiece. Don't you agree?"

"Well, yes, I imagine he would. But I don't really know his name or who he is yet."

The man's mouth fell open and he stuttered. "I'm..I'm...s...sorry, Miss. I...I don't understand. You've bought an expensive pocket watch for someone you don't know?"

Julia sighed. She shouldn't have said anything.

"Please just use the words I gave you."

The man nodded and regarded Julia with an expression of suspicious curiosity, a look one might give a person in an asylum.

"How long will it take?"

"For the engraving? Ten days. Sorry, Miss, but you won't have it in time for Christmas."

"That's all right." Julia turned and walked a few steps

and heard the salesman mumble, "Now there's an odd girl. Buying a gift for someone she doesn't know. Tsk tsk."

Shrugging, she checked her wristwatch and hurried out of the store to begin the three-block walk to her trolley stop. If she didn't get there in time for the five p.m. streetcar, she would be waiting half an hour.

This year Julia was determined that she would meet her beloved, the man for whom she had been praying these past four years. Why hadn't she met him yet? Some of her friends were already married. Her beloved *was* out there and she *would* find him. Yes, 1918 would also be the year that she would meet her beloved.

Each December, Julia wondered what she would buy her beloved for Christmas. Last year, she searched different stores but found nothing special. She finally discovered — and bought — a brown leather pocket journal at a specialty store at Broad and Bigler Streets. She didn't know whether her beloved would be the sort to write in one, but it seemed like an appropriate gift, especially since it had a delicate leaf embossed on the cover. The year before, she had bought a sterling silver Miraculous Medal because her beloved would be Catholic.

That first year, her mother suggested that she begin praying for her future husband. After a few weeks of doing so, Julia felt inspired to do more. It had been the week before Christmas, so she decided that she would buy or make him a Christmas gift each year until they met. With no job and no money that year, Julia knit him two pairs of socks, one blue-green and one green-brown, with finely-made yarn that her mother had given her.

The fact that she had made or bought gifts, and had spent hard-earned money for her future husband, had not pleased her father as he thought it too impractical and sentimental. Her mother, however, had declared that it was a beautiful gesture. Of course, if Mother knew how much she had spent on the most recent gift, she was pretty certain her mother wouldn't be happy.

The dinging of the trolley bell prompted Julia to rush across the street just as the trolley was pulling to a stop. She stepped onto the car and dropped the tokens into the box. The motorman called, "Next stop, 10th and Market."

On this particular day, Ann Fremont, Julia's closest friend, had left work early, so Julia took the streetcar home alone. Besides, Ann had been too anxious to be of much company these days since her beau, Theo, had just been shipped overseas. And just before Christmas. Ann had every reason to be afraid for him.

The two girls had met at Catholic Girls High School and had graduated in 1915. They had both likewise gotten their first jobs at Horn and Hardart's Automat in Center City, Julia as a sandwich maker and Ann as a pie maker.

Ann was especially supportive of Julia's idea to buy gifts for her beloved. "That's so romantic," she had said.

Years ago, Julia had written down a complete list of attributes her beloved would have: blue eyes, blond hair, ruddy but clear complexion, handsome and, of course, he would be tall and broad-shouldered. She had always favored men with light hair to contrast her own poker-straight dark hair. Most importantly, her beloved would be kind and gentlemanly, with a calm disposition, and he would never lose his temper. It would, of course, be "love at first sight." And there would be *no* doubt.

Admittedly, she should've met her beloved by now. God had already chosen her beloved, she reminded herself as she gazed out the trolley window. She only needed to be patient. Yes, 1918 would be *the* year. She was certain of that.

***

Soissons, France

Another Christmas in this hellhole of a war. The motorcar bounced in and out of holes on a rural dirt road near Soissons, France. Major Peter Winslow gripped the steering wheel as he made his way to the Vauxbuin Field Hospital nearby. It was snowing — again. Back home in Canada, he enjoyed snowshoeing, skiing and ice skating. But here, in the context of the war, snow was more an annoyance than anything.

Peter had joined the 38th Battalion of the Canadian Expeditionary Forces in Ottawa the summer of last year when he had turned 22. At that time, he had already achieved two post-secondary degrees from McGill University, one in French Literature and one in German Literature. He had even developed an affinity for writing sonnets, in English, though.

He remembered how exuberant he was to fight in the war overseas, especially when his older brother, John, had joined the same battalion months previous.

Cheeky. Pompous. Overconfident. He and his fellow Canadian, Australian and British soldiers had no idea what war entailed. And this war was worse than other wars if one considered the modern weapons of gas and airplanes. This "Great War" — or now that the Americans had joined, this "World War" — was supposed to be easy. Two-and-a-half years later, this "war to end all wars" still raged on with no end in sight. The devastating Halifax explosion earlier this month didn't help the morale of the Canadian soldiers, either.

Peter drove at dusk, thankful that the light of the moon illuminated the dirt road.

The brisk December winds cut into his face and he stiffened. Biting winds were the least of his problems. As a French and German translator for the Allied Forces, Peter often had to travel through dangerous areas close to the front or into *no man's land*. His orders this evening were to proceed to the field hospital, interrogate the lone German officer, then escort him to the POW camp in Pommiers across the Aisne River — if the prisoner was well enough to travel.

During the past year and a half, there were times Peter wanted to climb the closest hilltop and scream. Most days, though, he merely tried to make it through each week alive, wishing — praying — that this wretched war would soon end. The Americans were finally here, but he had yet to actually meet any. President Wilson had wanted to stay out of the war, despite the begging from the Allies. Peter understood their reticence: many Americans came from immigrant families with German relatives; some had roots in Allied France, Ireland or England. Even so, while he was now relieved that the Americans had joined the war effort, Peter wondered whether it might be too little — or too late.

One thing was certain: he would never, ever take his family for granted again. His one saving grace was that his older brother John was stationed here in France, and they had been fortunate to spend a weekend together in Paris eight months ago when there had been a lull in the fighting. John had looked weary, almost ragged, so Peter hated saying goodbye to him.

"Pete, take care of Mum and Dad if something happens to me over here."

"*Nothing's going to happen to you.*"

He nodded, his eyes cast downward. "You're probably right, but I have a bad feeling, like I'm not going to see them again."

"*You will. Stop all the gloom and doom talk. Let's have dinner.*"

Of course, Peter understood his brother's feeling of foreboding. Everyone over here — soldiers, nurses, the French civilians — understood it. For Peter, the only thing that kept him optimistic in the beginning were Lucy's cheerful letters. Lucy McCann had been the loveliest girl in Arnprior, Ontario. He found time to write several sonnets for her in the first six months of the war. Alas, she had waited until that Christmas of 1916 to send him a letter informing him of her engagement and upcoming marriage to a chap named Elliot. *Nice Christmas gift.* Peter had felt betrayed, but he had decided that he would not give her another thought. *Easier said than done.* And now, a year later, he occasionally thought about her — and had even kept her picture — although he hadn't been able to compose one poem since.

His kid sister, 15-year-old Maggie, shared with him in her last letter that Lucy had just given birth to her first child, a boy, and that she looked "dreadful." Peter wanted to hug his sister. She knew what to say in her letters to make him smile. Although his family was well off, his diminutive mother and his shy and unassuming 20-year-old sister, Dorothy — known as Dot — had just started working at a local factory making blankets for the soldiers. His father continued running the family insurance company, but he also volunteered by assisting local farmers whose sons were serving overseas.

Peter was no longer a church-going man, although he still believed in God. In fact, he had begged God for the past three months to end this awful war so he could return to his family and to his normal life in his hometown of Arnprior, a small logging town in the Ottawa Valley. He especially felt their absence during the holiday season.

Christmas at the Winslow household entailed some of the most tantalizing foods in the Valley: Grand-mère's tourtière, turkey with all the trimmings, Mum's delicious fruit cake and shortbread cookies. Maggie would sing "O Holy Night" with the voice of an angel while Dot played the piano. His father rarely laughed, but Pop's smile could melt the hardest of hearts. Together with their neighbours, on Christmas Eve they would walk from house to house caroling up John Street, left on Madawaska Boulevard and then up Daniel Street, no matter how cold it was, no matter how heavy the snow was falling. Then they would all attend Midnight Mass at St. John Chrysostom Church. *God, how I miss my family.*

Merry Christmas, Sir Robert Borden, as you enjoy your nice warm bed in the prime minister's house, sipping spiked eggnog and singing Christmas carols.

He shook his head, scowling. After a moment, Peter softened. He had it better than most soldiers. However, he had seen enough death and dismemberment to last a hundred lifetimes. *Please, God, end this war soon. Allow me to spend next Christmas at home.*

Chapter 2
Off to France

March 20th, 1918

A strong gust of wind nearly knocked Julia over, so she grasped onto Ann's arm as they strolled up Chestnut Street towards Broad. Julia's mother had asked her to buy three balls of yarn at a small shop near City Hall on her way home from work this evening.

As they approached Broad Street, they paused to watch the marching of the troops and hundreds of newly-enlisted men singing "Over There." Passersby joined in and soon the patriotic voices of civilians and soldiers made Julia feel proud to be an American. According to Julia's father and most gentlemen, since the United States joined the Allies last year, the war would only last a few more months.

Ann yanked on Julia's coat and pointed to a sign on the sidewalk. "Look, Jules, the Red Cross is recruiting medical aid workers. Training provided." The next thing Julia knew, the two young women were inside. There didn't seem to be any pause, just wide eyes and a nod. Before they knew it, they had both signed their names on the form to enlist. It was as if the entire scene played out like a moving picture, with Julia watching the events unfold in front of her. It seemed so right and natural, as if her entire life was meant for this moment: to join the war effort, with enthusiasm, and to minister to the sick and wounded.

As she sat beside Ann on the trolley, Julia studied her friend. Ann's light brown hair always shimmered and her green eyes seemed to change color, depending on her mood. Ann chattered on about Europe and how she had never been anywhere except for the Jersey shore and New York City, and how maybe she would see Theo and her brother. Her friend's animated speech became background noise as Julia wondered how her parents would react to her enlistment. She suddenly dreaded telling them. But she was, after all, 21. Julia could make these decisions of her own volition.

That evening, when she informed her parents that she had enlisted as a medical aid worker, her mother seemed almost ambivalent, then she smiled widely. Her father, normally strong and stoic, had tears in his eyes. But her mother nodded. "Yes, this is a good way for our family to support the war effort since your father's too old and your brothers are too young."

Julia was surprised that her mother seemed so agreeable. She had half-expected Mother to encourage her to sell Liberty bonds or knit for the troops. Instead, her mother kept nodding, then dialed the telephone to proudly inform everyone in the family — and the neighborhood — that her daughter "was enlisting" in the war effort.

As Julia lay in bed trying to drift off to sleep, she felt the full weight of her decision. Her imagination conjured up all sorts of images: attending to wounded soldiers on battlefields, holding bandaged heads to moisten parched lips with water, reading to soldiers, writing letters. Maybe she *would* meet her beloved on the battlefields of France. The more she thought about it, the more the enlistment felt right. Perhaps she hadn't met her beloved because she hadn't ventured anywhere outside of the Greater Philadelphia area and the Jersey shore.

After tossing and turning, she got out of bed and knelt beside her large wooden chest under the window sill. Raising the lid, she reached inside for the small cedar box containing the socks, journal, medal and the pocket watch, still wrapped carefully in cloth. Julia gingerly lifted out each item as if it was a fragile piece of glass. Her beloved would be pleased with these gifts; she was certain of that. Carefully placing her treasured items back into the box, she decided that this small box and her beloved's gifts would accompany her to France.

***

The following week, Julia and Ann attended the training session for new volunteers. They met and befriended Charlotte Zielinski from nearby Camden, New Jersey, an affable girl with brown hair, green eyes and an animated personality.

The training session's medical aspects included only how to properly put on a gas mask. While they learned when they would be departing and the sort of items they should pack, there was little to do with medical duties. Julia was disappointed, although she understood that they would not be considered formal "nurses," given that they had no medical training. Their responsibilities weren't the most important ones of the war, but she nonetheless prepared herself to bring meaning to these lesser duties.

Her family, as well as Ann's parents, accompanied the two girls by train to New York City and to the dock where they bid their daughters farewell. Beside her, Ann's mother wept, and Julia found it hard to say her own goodbyes.

Her father finally embraced her. In his slight Irish accent said, "Stay safe, Jules. May the Blessed Virgin watch over you."

"Yes, Dad."

Her mother pursed her lips as she said goodbye, as if she regretted her agreeable — almost enthusiastic —

compliance to her daughter's enlistment. Mother then shoved something in Julia's palm and kissed her cheek. Opening her hand, Julia could see her mother's blue crystal rosary beads. She put them into her coat pocket. The family had begun reciting the Holy Rosary every evening since her parents had heard about the apparitions of Our Lady in Fatima, Portugal, the previous year. Admittedly, Julia often found her mind wandering during the Rosary. However, she found the repetitive prayers consoling and understood why her mother would want her to have the beads while she was in France.

Jack, her 16-year-old brother, already a head taller than Julia, bit down on his lip, trying hard not to cry, but her two youngest brothers sobbed openly. Joey, 11 years old and nearly the same size as Julia, wouldn't let go of her hand. Seven-year-old Jimmy, the smallest of her siblings, squeezed Julia until she forced herself to push away from him. "It'll be all right, Jimmy. The war will be over in a few months."

Jimmy sniffed and wiped his eyes with his hands. "How do you know, Jules?"

"I just do."

The girls made their way to the deck of the ship and waved goodbye to their families. Tears welled in Ann's eyes. Julia stifled back a sob. Neither girl had ever been away from their families for any length of time, let alone traveled to another continent. She put her arm around her friend — now partner — in this new adventure.

As the ship launched, the girls waved to their families below. Sailing across the harbor, the Statue of Liberty loomed large beside them. The two girls' chins lifted to take in the entire statue. Julia never realized how enormous the statue was, and she couldn't stop staring, her mouth open. "Better shut your mouth or you'll catch a fly," Ann whispered.

Gazing up at the statue again, she thought about the Emma Lazarus sonnet, "The New Colossus," written to raise money for the pedestal of the Statue of Liberty, and now engraved on a bronze plaque inside the base of the statue. She had to memorize it for history class when she was in high school.

"Give me your tired, your poor,
Your huddled masses yearning to breathe free,
The wretched refuse of your teeming shore.
Send these, the homeless, tempest-tost to me,
I lift my lamp beside the golden door!"

Although Julia had learned about the Statue of Liberty, she had never seen it. The massive reminder of American liberty took her breath away. As the steamer plowed through New York Harbor and continued to the ocean, the statue soon became a speck in the distance.

Later that day, they joined their new friend, Charlotte. Charlotte introduced them to an acquaintance of hers, Ella Neumann, a tall, thin woman with long, curly blond hair. Ella spoke softly as she explained that she was a trained nurse and was being summoned to replace a nurse at the American Hospital in Le Tréport, situated near the water in Northern France. At 24, Ella was older than the three volunteers. Julia learned that Ella had three younger siblings like herself.

The ship's very cramped and crowded sleeping quarters meant little privacy for the girls, but they were all so excited about their trip to Europe that their chatter continued into the wee hours of the night. Charlotte, with her hands moving as she spoke, entertained Julia and the other volunteers with her wit and humor. She also played the violin — unfortunately, out of tune. Three of the girls had asked Charlotte to put away her violin. Julia didn't mind hearing her play because Charlotte seemed to be enjoying herself.

Three days into the voyage, the mood on board changed when most of the passengers came down with seasickness. Her friends Ann, Charlotte and Ella had retreated to the cabins below deck since they were all vomiting. Julia had tried to comfort the girls, but they all insisted that she leave.

Julia had always been blessed with a strong stomach. While most were in their cabins, she and a handful of male soldiers remained on deck.

Her thoughts wandered to her beloved. Could he, in fact, be here on this ship? Maybe *at this very moment*? She scanned the men and decided that no, her beloved was certainly *not* among this somber crew. She remained seated in a deck chair, reading a handbook on nursing and eating a Hershey's chocolate bar. Then, realizing she hadn't recited her prayers, she took out her mother's blue rosary and began praying.

***

The stench of vomit permeated the sleeping cabins the following morning, so Julia woke earlier than expected. Besides, the retching of so many girls in the sleeping quarters during the night made Julia keep a pillow over her head.

The next day, the rough seas finally abated and the steamer landed in Bordeaux.

Chapter 3
Sleeping Men

Soissons, France
April 13, 1918

Peter sipped black coffee and bit into his croissant. Earlier this morning, he had listened to intercepted radio messages from Austria-Hungary and Germany. Later on, he would be interrogating an enemy officer.

The croissants made his duties tolerable. Even with the food shortages, Madame Delacroix baked the flakiest and most mouth-watering croissants he had ever tasted. Madame was a large-boned elderly woman with hair pulled back so tightly that she had no wrinkles and eyes that could express every emotion. Each day that Peter was in Soissons, she brought croissants to him and Corporal Smythe. Her middle-aged son, André, once worked at the Allied office in Soissons and she always brought enough croissants for her son, Peter and Corporal Smythe. Unfortunately, earlier this year, a roadside bombing had killed André. Madame still brought the croissants every day. Peter suspected that the woman worked through her grief by baking.

He especially enjoyed conversing with her in her native language, and she seemed to appreciate it. Linguistically, he preferred his maternal grandmother's mother tongue, French — even above English.

Peter yearned for a few quiet days to catch up on correspondence and other personal duties. Yesterday, he received another letter from Maggie — how he enjoyed his sister's notes. Her frequent mail always brought a smile to his face.

Easter Sunday came and went two weeks ago. It was no different than any other day. Church wasn't something that interested him these days.

His brother John attended every Mass or service offered in the battlefields, trenches or churches. John had written to him several months ago, informing him of his planned leave in Paris over the Easter weekend and attempting to entice Peter to apply for leave at the same time. As much as he would have liked to, he couldn't, given the recent Battle of Rosières where the Huns captured a communications centre at Montdidier. Many of the messages intended for that centre were being transferred to his smaller command post, and there was no time for leave.

Of course, he knew that John had ulterior motives for visiting Paris. Last time he wrote, he shared that he had met a lovely girl named Laura who was a telephone operator.

Peter sat back in his chair, thinking of the last time they visited Paris a year ago. His brother was less talkative than usual, no doubt due to what they had both experienced and seen in this place. He wished he could visit with his brother this weekend, maybe even take in a cabaret show. Of course, his brother would never consider going to the cabarets or watching half-naked women. Instead, John would be planning to attend church for the Paschal Triduum. Peter admired his older brother's strong faith.

As Peter relaxed in his chair, he reminded himself to be grateful that he was no longer in the trenches. In the beginning, as a Canadian non-commissioned officer, he spent the first four months in the trenches and on the front lines until a deep shrapnel wound in his foot, as well as trench foot, sent him to an Army field hospital. Lying beside two German soldiers in the ambulance and pretending to be unconscious, Peter listened as they whispered in German about how they would kill the driver and the two other wounded soldiers on board. He was in tremendous pain from the shrapnel wound, but he had no choice. Before they could strike, Peter calmly, secretly and carefully got his pistol ready. As soon as one soldier crept forward to kill the driver, Peter jumped into action, and said in German, "I wouldn't do that if I were you." The man turned and pointed his pistol at Peter. He shot the soldier, then held the gun on the other man. He despised killing, but it was either him or the soldier. Peter was hailed as a hero. He received a commendation and a promotion to Major. After his recuperation, he was offered a job in the translation department of the Allied Forces.

He was currently stationed in Soissons at the communications centre, on the second floor of a bank on Boulevard Jeanne d'Arc.

"Major Winslow, telegram for you." Corporal Smythe held out a paper. The man was slight and fair-haired as well as soft-spoken. He didn't fill the air with useless words, and he was one of the most responsible and dependable men Peter had ever worked with.

"Thank you, Corporal."

He broke open the envelope, tensing as he read the telegram. *"The Canadian Army regrets to inform you that your brother, Sergeant John Leslie Winslow, was killed at St-Gervais-et-St-Protais Church in Paris as the result of German artillery fire on March 29th at 3:30 p.m. He was buried in a military cemetery nearby. For the location, read below."*

Peter shook his head and clenched his fists. *Well, isn't that just perfect?* His brother killed, not in the line of fire, not in a battle, not in defence of his country but in a bloody church. Where did his brother's devout faith get him? Killed. In a church. Worshipping the very God who was supposed to protect him.

Peter blew out a sigh. He was a soldier, an officer, for crying out loud. He would *not* show his emotion. Not here. Not now.

The irony of it had not escaped him. Not only had God disregarded his prayers, God hadn't answered John's prayers or their saintly mother's prayers, the woman who prayed daily for her sons' safety. He crumpled, then pitched the paper across the room and swore.

No doubt he would be expected to compose the telegram that would devastate his parents and sisters. He had already written dozens of those letters, but he hadn't done so in over a year. It was a job he despised. His heart ached thinking of what he must tell his family. They would be inconsolable.

Peter kicked the side of his desk, immediately regretting it. Sharp pain, then throbbing, took over. His injured foot would never be the same. Scarring and pain were daily reminders. He didn't want to deal with death anymore. He didn't want to think about the fact that his brother was gone.

He wiped the beginnings of tears from his eyes and focused his attention on the dreadful telegram. He dipped the pen into the ink and wrote the words for the telegram. He hated this damn war. He hated that so many had to die. Besides, John was the *good* son. *Why couldn't I have died?*

April 13, 1918

Dearest Mum, Dad, Dot and Maggie,

I have dreadful news to tell and there is no way of softening the blow. John has been killed.

Peter pressed hard into the paper, then threw the pen across the room and swore. He ripped the paper to shreds. He began to shake, then weep.

Knocking at his door competed with his grief. "Sir, sir?" came a voice.

"Leave me alone!" he yelled, as he heard the door open.

"Yes, sir. Sorry, sir."

Sniffing, Peter wiped his eyes with the back of his hand, then took out a fresh piece of paper. He must finish this without delay. He straightened and closed his eyes. Proceeding without haste, Peter carefully composed the words that would forever change his family.

***

After billeting with French families in Bordeaux, the girls traveled by train to Paris. Julia and the others received orders to proceed immediately to the front.

Julia, Charlotte, Ann and most of the other female volunteers were directed to climb into a covered *camion* to travel to a field hospital. They were given uniforms, which they placed into their suitcases.

Ella would be traveling by train to Le Tréport to the American-run stationary hospital there. It was difficult for the girls to bid goodbye to their new friend, but they exchanged hugs and wished each other good luck.

As the truck bounced and swayed back and forth on the

dirt roads, Charlotte and Ann joked about their good fortune of getting to the front so soon. On the one hand, Julia felt that it was callous to be excited. On the other, it *was* exciting, and her hands shook and her heart raced. What would greet her and the rest of the girls when they arrived?

They found no seats in the *camion*, and judging from the foul stench, it had recently transported livestock. The girls were told to change into their uniforms on the way to the hospital. Every time the truck bounced, their suitcases slid across the floor like discs on a backgammon board. The girls slipped and fell as the truck moved along. Charlotte called out, *"C'est la guerre!"*

Julia looked forward to wearing the uniform and felt it important, despite the stench of the truck and the joviality of the others, that she look her best when she arrived at the field hospital. There were no mirrors in the *camion*, but she dressed in the uniform, taking special care to place on her head the veil of crisp white organdie with the Red Cross embroidered on the front.

Three hours later, they arrived near the city of Soissons, where a field hospital had been set up near a beautiful stone *château*. Dusk made it difficult to see and a soft rain had begun falling. Popping, like fireworks, in the distance greeted the young women as they filed out. Tent barracks lined the lawn near the stone castle, and Julia estimated the tents were large enough to hold forty or fifty cots each. Sleeping men covered the lawn. There had to be hundreds of them.

Inside the *château*, the girls were assigned a barrack in which to work and a cot on the third floor in which to sleep. After hastily putting their suitcases beside their cots, they were given bitter-tasting coffee and *croissants*, then told to proceed to their assigned barracks to begin working.

The British nurse in charge was a tall, middle-aged woman named Sister Agnes, and she quickly explained that nurses in Europe were referred to as "Sisters." Sister Agnes informed them that the "sleeping men" on the lawn were those wounded who needed treatment and that some would be dead before they made it into the barracks. When a few girls gasped, Sister Agnes calmed them. "This is war, young ladies. Be prepared to experience death many times each day. We cannot save every soldier who comes to us, but we can save *some*."

Standing beside Ann and Charlotte, Julia's heart felt heavy at the thought of all those men — hundreds — on the lawn, in pain, some dying, exposed to rainy, damp and cold weather.

Sister Betty gave them both name tags, then said, "Come along." When the girls hesitated, she yelled, "Now!"

Julia and Ann were given orders to proceed to Barrack 42. They bid goodbye to Charlotte, promising to see her sometime later.

Chapter 4
Baptism by Fire

It was now mid-afternoon, and while walking to the barracks, Julia and Ann had to swerve out of the way as stretcher-bearers carried wounded into a barrack ahead.

From the outside, Barrack 42 appeared to be a peaceful building. Ann opened the door slowly but could not push it more than half a foot, so she squeezed through, then motioned for Julia to come ahead.

Inside the building, however, confusion, pandemonium and disorder reigned. Cries, moans, shouts and orders from nurses and aides flew back and forth. Only dim flickers from candles and a few gas lamps illuminated the chaos. Julia realized that part of a cart had blocked the entrance, so she moved it to allow the door to be more accessible.

Cots were everywhere and not the 40 or so she imagined when she first saw these outbuildings. Instead, there were 60 or more, most cots close enough that the wounded could touch one another. The narrow door flung open. Julia and Ann jumped out of the way. Stretcher-bearers burst into the room carrying wounded soldiers, a steady stream of men, unconscious or moaning.

"You two, over here!" yelled a large buxom British nurse. "You," she pointed at Ann, "report to Sister Kate in the corner over there."

"You," she said to Julia, "tetanus shots. Here."

Julia read the woman's name tag, "Sister Betty," and

replied, "Yes, Sister." After all the anticipation, Julia was excited to begin working.

The large nurse pointed at the men on stretchers lining the south wall of the barracks. She thrust a basket with long hypodermic needles and packets of liquid in Julia's hand, then told her to give one to every wounded man along the wall. Once finished, she was to write a T on the man's forehead. *Lord in heaven*. Julia had no idea how to give a hypodermic, and how would she write on their foreheads?

She stood motionless for a moment and searched the area with her eyes to find someone who might help. Finally, amidst the chaos, another medical volunteer, a pretty dark-haired woman, smiled at her, then motioned for her to crouch down beside the first stretcher.

The girl snapped the glass tube containing the medicine, filled the syringe, then jabbed the needle in. Julia winced. "Good luck," the girl said in what sounded like a British accent.

"Wait."

The girl turned.

"How do I write a T on their forehead?"

"Be creative." She rushed off.

Taking a deep breath, Julia snapped the glass tube, filled the syringe then finally looked down at the man on the stretcher. He was unconscious, thank goodness, but when she plunged the needle in his thigh, the man moaned. All of a sudden, tiny bugs scurried all over the man's leg. "Ew!" Julia backed away. *Lice*. She had read that soldiers in the trenches were plagued with lice, but seeing it firsthand was revolting.

"Sorry," she whispered. Taking a bit of blood from his chest wound, she marked a T on his forehead.

Over the next five hours, Julia lost count of the number of men she had injected. Just when she had finished one row, the men were taken away and another row of stretchers arrived.

Before she gave another soldier a hypodermic, Sister Betty called for her to proceed to the opposite side of the room and "prepare men for the operating theater."

If she thought giving hypodermics was a challenge, preparing wounded men would turn out to be a much greater one. She watched another volunteer undress a British soldier, removing his clothing, boots, leggings, belt, gas mask and kit bag. Lice made a valiant effort to escape, but the girl sprayed something on the man first — hopefully to kill the lice — then she washed the soldier's body wounds as well as she could. The girl wrapped him in a clean sheet, leaving the clothes in a heap in the aisle.

"What did you spray on his body?"

"Naphthalene. It's supposed to kill them. But as you'll see, it's hard to get rid of all of them. Just a part of war, I suppose."

Now it was Julia's turn. Judging by the uniform, the first man she worked on was a German soldier. Thankfully, he wasn't conscious. Her hands trembled. She pulled at the sodden boots and uniform. His clothes were caked in mud and, as she removed them, the man mumbled something in German. She soaked the sponge in water, then tried to wash his legs. The caked-on mud had hardened like rock onto the man's skin. She scrubbed as best she could, all the while trying not to breathe through her nose. There was yellow pus and a putrid stench coming from the man's stomach wounds.

Whenever she saw lice — which was often — she used the spray.

Julia became better at her task as the hours passed. She found if she squeezed a bit of water on the mud-hardened skin before trying to rub, the mud was easier to remove.

The next three men had tiny leaf logos on their collars. The third one was wide awake, watching her struggle to remove the damp mud-caked clothing. Second-degree burns covered his leg from mid-thigh to calf. Avoiding eye contact, she asked, "So where are you from, sir?"

"Saskatoon."

Julia had never heard of such a place. "Where is that?"

"Canada."

The only thing she knew about Canada was that it was the country north of the United States. And it was cold.

Keeping her eyes focused on her task, she whispered, "I'm dreadfully sorry if I am hurting you." As she pulled the last bit of pant from him, some of his skin came off with it, and he drew in a breath. After cleaning him as gently as she could, she wrapped him in a fresh linen sheet, patted his arm and moved on to the next gentleman.

Moving to the next man, she winced when she saw that in place of his chest was a wide open hole. She had an unusually strong stomach, but seeing this man's torso torn open, both lungs exposed and slowly moving in and out, made her stop and stare, her heart racing in her own chest.

Shaking her head to get control of herself, she finally started to remove his clothes, all the while keeping her eyes fixed on the man's lungs moving in, out. As she inched his boot from his foot, his lungs became still. Julia's eyes glistened. This poor man was gone. Placing a sheet over his head, she prayed. *Almighty Father, have mercy on this man's soul.*

Steeling herself, she soon discovered that if the soldiers were conscious and they were Allied soldiers, the men were often talkative, afraid, but grateful for her help. One French soldier tried to speak to her, but her French was minimal, at best. The Germans were not as talkative, except for one boy of no more than sixteen, nearly the same age as her brother Jack. He spoke in broken English, his v's sounding like w's and his th's like z's. "I remember as a boy I visit uncle and cousins in Kansas. Americans good people. But as a man, I must fight for the Fatherland."

He was so free with his speech that Sister Betty came over and whispered, "Remember everything he says. The liaison officer may want to know what he communicated to you." Communicated to her? He was merely talking about his relatives in Kansas. Why would the small talk of a teenager interest anyone?

Julia became faster at her new task and by late afternoon, she could finally look each conscious man in the eye. But what she saw made her heart sink. She pursed her lips and continued working.

Later that afternoon, another group of men was brought in. Suffering from gas burns, these poor souls screamed, moaned and mumbled incoherent babble. One French soldier had large open blisters covering his chin, neck and chest. Julia had heard about mustard gas, but seeing gas wounds firsthand made her want to run in the opposite direction.

She had only been here for six hours. Julia shook her head. How could she — or would she — ever be the same?

Chapter 5
A Rough Beginning

Dearest Mum, Dad, Dot and Maggie,

It is with the most profound regret that I must inform you of John's death two weeks ago, on Good Friday, in St-Gervais-et-St-Protais Church in Paris by German artillery fire.

John was buried in a military cemetery near Paris. I will do my best to obtain a photograph so you may see his final resting place.

My love and sorrow to you all.

Your affectionate son,
Peter

He cringed. With his foot injury, warm socks became as necessary as a warm coat. Unfortunately, the socks he wore had seen better days and were nearly threadbare. Maggie had told Peter in her last letter that Mum had knit him two pairs of socks, but they had yet to arrive.

Peter could bear the pain in his foot. But his heart felt like a huge gaping wound. Earlier today, he had dozed off in his chair and had dreamt about John. He and his brother were standing in a church and a huge beam had dropped down upon Peter's legs. John removed the heavy piece of wood only to have the roof collapse on top of both of them. He had woken with a gasp, sweating. Blowing out a sigh, he fixed his gaze on the two reports in front of him on the desk.

Quiet knocking on his door made him look up. Smythe

avoided eye contact. "I'm sorry for whatever news you have received."

Peter could only nod. "My brother. Killed."

"Very sorry for your loss, sir."

"Thank you."

"I apologize for interrupting, but..."

"Yes?"

"We've received notice that Captain Reiniger, the high-ranking German officer, is at the field hospital, and you're to interrogate him there."

"Yes, of course. Corporal?"

"Yes, sir?"

"Take this to the Allied telegram office down the street immediately."

"Right away, sir."

In the motorcar, Peter refocused, driving slowly and keeping his attention fixed on the road ahead of him for any movement, land mines or possible dangers. He felt a special responsibility to stay alive now that his brother was gone. It was dusk, the best time to travel. While it had been quiet for a day or so, he had no reason to assume the next few days would be without incident.

***

Julia had just started to take a soldier's shirt off when she heard a voice behind her. "Wait."

Turning, Sister Betty pointed. "Prepare this man immediately. He's a German commanding officer. Major Winslow will be here soon to interrogate him."

Julia nodded and performed her task as directed. Thankfully, this blond-haired, blue-eyed man wasn't caked in mud. He was awake, watching her with no hint of a smile or frown. This particular German was not as chatty as the fellow she had treated a few hours earlier. He had brass buttons, buckles with black eagles, decorations, field glasses, fur-lined gloves, varnished boots and a shiny elegant helmet with a spiked top. The deep wound down the side of his leg would need stitching, but it was definitely not the sort of life-threatening wounds she had found on men she had treated earlier.

"What is taking so long, for crying out loud?"

Startled by a gruff voice, Julia turned to see an average-looking, dark-haired man in an officer's uniform. He was scowling.

"N...no, sir. He has all these extra — I still need to — finish..."

"I don't have all day. I need him ready immediately!" The man raised his voice. He spoke perfect English but with a peculiar accent.

"Sorry, Major," Sister Betty apologized. "This is one of our new American girls. It's her first day. I will help her."

Julia stole a glance in his direction only to find his jaw rigid, his mouth in the thin line of a frown.

On the verge of tears, Julia lifted her chin, took a deep breath and bit her lip to hold the tears at bay. She would *not* break down in front of this awful man. Wasn't he supposed to be on their side? And didn't he know what she had just been through on her very first day here?

***

Peter's first impression of the American girl was that she was painfully slow at her task. Good Lord, why couldn't they have given a more experienced girl the task of preparing this man for the operating theater?

He shrugged. Peter was glad the Yanks were finally here, but he didn't like their attitudes and found them a pompous lot, the few with whom he had any dealings. They seemed to think the war would end only because they were here. That ridiculous "Over There" song made him want to slap the next Yank who sang it. *And we won't stop there till it's over, over there.* Really? He shook his head.

Finally, Sister Betty assisted the girl and hastily wrapped a sheet around the German officer. The prisoner was taken by stretcher to the corner of the barrack behind a dressing screen.

In German, Peter asked, "State your name."

The prisoner responded, in German, "65739."

"Name?"

"65739."

Peter clenched his fists. He would like nothing better than to punch this smug blond-haired, blue-eyed enemy in the jaw. "Look, I know who you are. I have a photograph. You're Kapitän Reiniger, commanding officer of the German Imperial Army."

"65739."

"Fine. Don't answer any questions. I will return in three days' time and take you to a prisoner of war camp and interrogate you there. And I *will* get the answers to my questions by any means possible."

Kapitän Reiniger stared straight ahead.

"Make sure this prisoner is restrained," he called to Sister Betty.

Peter stormed out of the barrack and bumped into a girl. "Pardon me," he said, looking down again into the face of the slow American girl. Was that fear on her face? Peter didn't have time for skittish young girls with their clumsiness or their naïveté.

The girl pursed her lips, her eyes glistening.

Peter stopped, put his hands on his hips and looked down at her. "Look, I apologize, Miss, but you need to watch where you're going."

***

Julia blew out a breath. She would not allow this man to crush her spirit on an already difficult day. Julia watched the officer leave the building.

"Excuse me, Miss?" A feminine voice called to her.

She felt a hand on her shoulder and turned. Before her stood the pretty dark-haired girl who had shown her how to give a hypodermic. Her eyes were kind, but they told Julia that she had been through too much in her young life. She was dressed similarly to Julia with a blue skirt and blouse and a white apron, but with no Red Cross on her veil.

"Yes?"

"Major Winslow is not normally that cross." The girl replied in excellent English with a slight British accent. "He's one of the few officers around here who is very kind and considerate."

"Well, he certainly wasn't very considerate today."

"War can do that, Miss..."

"Murphy. Julia Murphy."

"I'm Madame Dubois. Thérèse, if you please."

Julia held out her hand. "Nice to meet you, ma'am. By the way, thank you for showing me how to give a hypodermic."

"My pleasure. And please call me Thérèse."

"Are you British?"

"Part British, part French. I live in Soissons with my twin girls, Sylvie and Sophie, as well as my mum. I'm a war widow. Lost my dear Pierre in the first year of the war."

"I'm so sorry."

Thérèse lowered her head. "Me, too."

"Your English is better than some Americans I know."

"My mother is British so I've been bilingual all my life. My girls are bilingual too."

"How many days a week do you work?"

"Three here at the field hospital. And it depends on the causalities, but usually one or two at St. Paul's Hospital in town."

"Well, it is good to meet you, Thérèse. Now, I suppose we'll have to get back to work."

Thérèse nodded. "Of course."

Chapter 6
River of Blood

In the ensuing never-ending three days, Julia crossed a river of blood so deep and so wide she wished that she could leave this awful place and never return. Not only was the physical work backbreaking, but there were few respites and rare opportunities for sleep. Julia hadn't yet become accustomed to the stench of blood. Nor would she ever become used to men with torn-off limbs, bodies burned from mustard gas, or shrapnel wounds wide enough to fit kit bags. These images now filled her vision nearly 24 hours a day. Sheer adrenaline and bitter-tasting coffee kept her going. Her tasks alternated between giving hypodermics and preparing men for the operating theater. She had no time to talk to Ann, Charlotte, her new friend Thérèse, or any other girls.

On the evening of the third night, sleep came immediately and ended too quickly when she woke to the sound of trucks bringing in more wounded. Barely able to move her limbs, she pushed herself up in bed. It felt like every bone in her body had been stretched through a wringer washer.

"Oh, every muscle in my body hurts." Ann stretched her hands in the air and looked across the room at Julia. "Where's Charlotte?"

Julia glanced at Charlotte's untouched bed. "Not sure. I don't even know where she's been working."

Other girls moaned and stretched, echoing their discomfort.

Downstairs in the first-floor dining hall, Sister Betty reminded Julia that Major Winslow would be arriving to pick up the German officer. At the mention of Major Winslow's name, Julia scowled. Sister Betty must have seen the look on Julia's face because she said — in her proper British accent — "Major Winslow's a fine man, an exceptional officer. Compared to most, he's still standing, still speaking coherently, and he does not have shell shock. Besides, the poor man just lost his brother."

Julia's shoulders sagged and her mood turned melancholic. How would she react if one of her beloved brothers had been killed? Suffice it to say, she might even be more caustic than the major had been.

Major Winslow certainly had his admirers. First, Thérèse, then Sister Betty. He was obviously well-liked.

"Sad, but all too common in this war. Finish your meal and return to your duties preparing the German officer."

After having a piece of cheese and a slice of bread, Julia headed back to Barrack 42.

Julia watched as a gray-haired Catholic priest dressed in a cassock went from soldier to soldier, anointing each man, making the sign of the cross and speaking to those who were conscious. He even stopped and spoke to the enemy soldiers. The priest paused at Kapitän Reiniger's cot. "Would you like —"

In English with a slight accent, Kapitän Reiniger interrupted by waving his hand to tell the priest to move on.

Then Kapitän Reiniger motioned for Julia to approach.

"I think I have enough time for...a shave," — he patted his cheeks —"before I leave."

"Uh, I'm not sure." She scanned the barrack looking for someone to ask, but everyone was busy. "I suppose it would be all right."

"Yes, a nurse was shaving a soldier earlier. The equipment is on the cart over there." He pointed.

Julia retrieved the shaving equipment and lathered the man's face. She took the razor and carefully slid it along his face. Kapitän Reiniger was a handsome man, even with the three days' growth of light beard on his face. Julia found herself daydreaming about this man's life, his family. Did he have a sweetheart who would be waiting for him to return home?

Suddenly, the man yanked the razor out of Julia's hand and sliced his throat, so deep that the now-exposed artery sprayed Julia and the cots around her in a shower of deep crimson.

"No!!" She pressed her hands on the gaping wound in his throat, but it was too late. Kapitän Reiniger died within seconds, and there was nothing Julia could do for him.

***

"What?" Peter yelled as he stared at the blood-soaked sheet covering the officer. Frustrated, he shot a glance upward. Then he did a double-take. Red streaks crisscrossed the ceiling of the barrack. "Whose idiotic idea was it to shave this prisoner? And didn't I tell you to restrain him?"

"The prisoner's idea," Sister Betty placated. "And, yes, you did, but as you can see, it's total chaos in here. Besides, our new American girl did not know the protocol.

Sorry, Major. The girls and I have had little sleep."

His jaw hardened. "'Sorry' does not bring back this man, Sister. He was the commanding officer of three divisions." He lifted his foot to kick the cot, then reconsidered and pulled it back. Slamming his foot against the metal would just aggravate his already throbbing foot. He stared downward.

"Your foot's still bothering you?"

"When it's damp, which has been every day."

"Dr. Kilgallen can take a look at it. Come back in a few days and allow him to check it out."

He sighed. "Maybe. Thank you, Sister."

***

Julia could hear Major Winslow yelling from across the barrack. She had no intention of interacting with that man this afternoon, so she crouched behind a cart, hoping the major wouldn't see her. Thérèse, who was cleaning a soldier nearby, glanced at her with concern. Julia forced a smile and pointed at the major. Thérèse nodded.

She scrubbed and washed her hands with a strong-smelling soap for at least 15 minutes and she still couldn't remove all the blood from under her fingernails. Worse, she could still smell his blood on her apron.

Guilt already tortured Julia's soul. She had no idea that Kapitän Reiniger would grab the razor to harm himself. *I just wanted to help a wounded soldier.* Truth be told, she hadn't even recognized the razor as a weapon. When Julia's father was ill last year, she would help shave his face. She'd never imagined a person would use it to hurt himself — especially in front of so many people.

These past three days had already been so

excruciatingly difficult without that soldier committing suicide in front of her.

She shook her head and pursed her lips. It was time to stop being naïve and gullible. This was not normal day-to-day living. In war, anything could happen. The sooner she embraced that notion, the better it would be for everyone.

Chapter 7
Wool Socks
and Leisure Time

April 18, 1918

"Sir?" Peter glanced up from his desk. Corporal Smythe stood in front of his desk. "You've...uh... received...a...letter, sir."

"Letter? Hand it over. From my family?" No doubt they now knew about John's passing.

"Uh, no, sir. It's...well, it's —" Smythe was an unassuming man but could be aggressive — and annoying — when necessary.

"Spit it out, Corporal. Who is it from?"

The man lowered his head, avoiding eye contact. He held the letter out. "Here."

Peter took hold of it and gasped when he saw the return address. *John Winslow, Paris.*

His heart pounded. His ears began to ring. Taking a deep breath, he released it in a long sigh, then ripped open the letter.

Paris, March 29, 1918

Dear Pete,

I nearly did not get my leave. It was splendid that I finally managed to, of course. A lot of action nearby, but thankfully, Paris seems to have escaped much of the devastation the rural areas of France have endured.

I told you that I met a girl. Laura works with the telephone company here and she's American! She and I will be attending Good Friday service as well as Easter Sunday at a beautiful church here with a long name.

Say, Pete, I think we're nearing the end of this thing and I'm confident it will be over soon. Can you just imagine sitting down to Mum's pot roast, listening to Maggie's antics and playing gin with Dot? Then heading off to watch a hockey game — or better yet — to skate on the frozen Madawaska this winter? Wouldn't that be keen?

Must write to Mum and Dad, Dot and Maggie.

Best,

John

Peter gingerly, reverently placed the letter on his desk. He blinked to keep the tears from forming. He tensed, then nodded. His family needed to have this letter, so he would forward it to them immediately.

***

The unending droves of wounded ceased abruptly. For two entire days, no new casualties arrived and nearly 30 men had been transferred to one of the stationary hospitals in northern France. Having more time and leisure, Julia relaxed on her cot and picked up the most recent letter from Jack.

Dearest Sister,

I hope you are keeping out of harm's way. We pray for you every night while we are reciting the Rosary. I do find myself envious of you, though. I can't tell you how much I want to be over there, fighting the Huns, fighting for my country. In only a year or so, I'll be old enough to enlist. How swell would that be? If the war lasts that much longer.

Julia stopped reading. How she wished she could tell him that *he* was the one to be envied. He could eat and sleep whenever he wanted and not see these horrible images on a daily basis. Then again, before she came here, Julia had also been excited to do her patriotic duty. She made a mental reminder to dissuade her brother's longings to fight in her next letter to him.

"Jules?"

She looked up to see Ann standing at the foot of her cot.

"Yes?"

"Want to explore the grounds and interior of the *château*?"

Julia placed the letter back into the envelope and slid it into her drawer. "That sounds wonderful!"

Until now, they had only seen the inside of two barracks, the dining area inside the *château* and their large sleeping quarters on the third — and highest — floor.

Outside, most of the "sleeping men" had been transferred to tents or brought inside the *château*. But the grass, still flattened, contained bits of human flesh and blood, and the girls tried to avoid stepping on them.

They reached the far side of the camp, where a narrow stream and a meadow stretched forth in front of them. The sun had disappeared behind the clouds but it was warmer than the previous few weeks. It started to drizzle, and a large maple tree invited the girls to take cover as they waited for the rain to cease.

The rain tapped the tree and ground, and the girls remained silent. Raining usually meant more mud-covered soldiers to care for, but she tossed that thought aside and took a deep breath, reveling in the scent of water-drenched earth.

Once the rain slowed to a mist, the girls returned to the *château*. This castle was not like the enormous ones she had seen in picture books. However, the building had high ceilings, colorful wallpaper and numerous large rooms. A steep staircase lined one wall of the wide foyer, leading to the upper rooms.

When they reached the second floor, Ann shook her head. "All of a sudden, I feel so fatigued. I don't think I shall ever catch up on sleep after the past few weeks."

"Me, too. But I don't know when we'll get another opportunity to explore this magnificent building."

"I'd rather sleep, Jules."

"Very well." They separated, with Ann continuing up the stairs to the sleeping quarters and Julia remaining to explore.

This floor contained the allied officers' convalescent ward. Stepping in, Julia noticed two men in front of the large window smoking pipes and two men asleep on their cots. The men glanced up and smiled. Julia returned the gesture then walked back into the hallway.

Beyond the officer's ward was another room where the door was slightly ajar.

She heard Dr. Kilgallen speaking with Sister Betty. Julia liked Dr. Kilgallen because he was younger than most of the doctors here and worked hard to save as many men — Allied and enemy — as he could.

"We haven't received the shipment of wool socks for the men yet, Sister. Perhaps we could ask the townspeople to donate wool socks. Many of the men have foot injuries."

"Our sock donation bin is nearly empty. And the people in Soissons barely have clothes to wear, sir. But it couldn't hurt to ask. One of our new girls knits. I'll ask her to knit a few pairs."

Soldiers were in need of wool socks?

As Julia started for the staircase, she stopped, her eyes wide. Wool socks? Of course! Julia already had two pairs of wool socks in her possession, socks that she knit years ago. But... those socks were for her beloved. Perhaps she should offer to donate only one pair?

She shook her head. There was only one thing to do. The socks should go to the donation bin. They should go to a needy soldier. Besides, it would be simple enough to knit two additional pairs of socks for her beloved at a later time.

Julia raced upstairs and to her cot. She might be able to place the socks in the bin immediately.

Gathering the socks from her small wooden box, Julia banged the small chest closed. Ann stirred in the cot near hers. "Jules? What's going on?"

"Nothing, go back to sleep. Everything's fine."

The girl nodded and rolled over, pulling her cover up to her chin.

Julia raced down the staircase, two pairs of socks in hand, and nearly ran into Sister Betty in the foyer.

"Sister?"

"Yes?"

"Where is the donation bin for wool socks for the soldiers?"

Sister Betty looked down at Julia's hands. "That's incredible."

"What?"

"Well, I was just saying to Dr. K...well, never mind. The donation bin is at the front desk." She pointed to the desk on the other side of the foyer. "You're either the fastest knitter I've ever seen or..."

"I'm not, Sister. I overheard you and Dr. Kilgallen talking about socks. I just happened to have two pairs with me."

"Two pairs of men's wool socks?"

"It's a long story. I'm happy to donate these."

"Marvelous. Actually, I'm heading to the desk now." She took the socks from Julia. As Julia turned to go, Sister said, "Wait. These are very finely made, Miss Murphy. And very unique. I'm sure they'll go to a soldier who needs them. Thank you."

"You're welcome, Sister." Julia returned to the barrack where she was working and felt light as air. A poor unfortunate soldier would soon be wearing these socks that she knit with her own hands. Peace and joy filled her soul.

***

Later that day, Peter stopped by Dr. Kilgallen's office as scheduled. Dr. K listened to his heart and took his blood pressure. Peter kept silent, but the overwhelming loss of his brother seemed too much to bear. These were the moments when he wished he had a girl in his life, someone with whom he could share his thoughts and who could make this lousy war bearable.

Dr. K asked Peter to take off his boot and sock. Then the doctor examined his foot. "I'm sorry to hear about your brother."

"Thank you."

"You know," Dr. K said, "this war is bad enough, but to lose your brother? Make sure you take care of yourself."

"I don't have time, Doc. Too much else on my mind. Like this foot."

"You must wear wool socks, Major. Your right foot needs to be kept as dry and warm as possible. Check the sock bin downstairs at the front desk."

"This foot will get better once the wretched war is over."

"Of course, it will. Remember...wool socks."

"Yes."

"Maybe you can find someone to write to. Some of the female volunteers have begun writing to the soldiers who have passed through here and are back on the battlefield. I bet it's good for their morale to get a cheery letter now and again, especially from a young lady."

Peter shrugged. "Maybe." He wasn't quite sure how he would go about acquiring a friendly correspondent, but the doctor was correct. It would definitely help if he received a cheery letter now and then. Maggie's letters had been few and far between sometimes since they were coming from Canada.

On his way out of the *château*, Peter stopped at the front desk and saw the metal bin containing only two pairs of socks. The pair on top was an interesting shade of blue-green and made with thinner wool, which was the sort he preferred. The other pair was made with similar wool but a green-brown colour. He picked one pair up, leaving the other pair inside for someone else. Just then, a nurse came out with a huge box.

"More socks in here, sir, if you'd like them."

"If there are more, then perhaps I shall take both of these pairs, if that is all right with you."

"Absolutely, sir. We've been waiting on wool socks for two weeks. I'm glad they finally arrived."

***

Julia dipped a sponge into a pan of water and looked up to see that cranky officer —Major Winslow — come inside the barrack. She turned toward the stretcher to squeeze out the sponge on the man's stomach and cleaned it as best she could. After she finished, she carried the basin to the back door.

She overheard the major speaking to Sister Gwen. Glancing in that direction, Julia just about dropped her basin. The socks she had knit — and had donated to some unfortunate soldier — were in his hands! How dare he take those socks. He was as fit as any soldier.

Julia took a deep breath and stomped out the back door, dumped the bin of water and returned. She would not allow that man to take the socks she had knit for her beloved and had donated to some poor unfortunate soldier. *No, sir.* Major Winslow may be an Allied officer, but he could not have those socks.

***

Socks in hand, Peter nodded as he listened to the nurse's report concerning the German officer who remained unconscious after having his right leg amputated. But the loss of a limb was not the man's only problem. Most of his left leg was burned and deep shrapnel wounds in his abdomen were infected. The nurse didn't expect him to live much longer. Peter bid the woman farewell, his cap under his arm, his new socks in hand, and turned to find the clumsy American girl standing in front of him.

"Sir?"

"Yes?"

She opened her mouth to speak, but nothing came out. She pursed her lips and finally said, "I wonder...well, I wonder... if I...well, might speak with you?"

Peter cocked his left eyebrow and almost smiled. The girl's mouth was pursed. Was she scowling? Despite the expression, this was the first time he had an opportunity to take a close look at the American girl. She was quite pretty, chocolate brown hair, pale skin. And her eyes were a deep dark brown that he could only describe as...intense. And *why* was she frowning?

He leaned forward. "Yes, Miss..."

"Uh...Murphy — Miss — Julia Murphy."

"Miss Julia Murphy. What can I do for you? I really do need to depart."

"I...well, I'd...." Miss Murphy bit down on her lip and glanced away.

He huffed, his hand on his hip. "Yes?"

"You...the socks. You took those socks... from the donation bin, didn't you?"

"So? What of it?"

"Those socks were meant to assist a poor unfortunate soldier. Not a man as fit as you." She stood, indignant, her hands on her hips, waiting for an answer.

"I beg your pardon. What are you talking about?"

"You got those socks from the donation bin."

"Well, Miss..." He stood taller and smirked. Where was this girl coming from? And why was she so offended that he had taken these socks?

"Because Dr. Kilgallen told me to take them. If you must know, my foot suffers from a two-year-old injury. And might I say that I was serving the Allied Forces at the time. But *why* would it matter to you that I took these socks?"

"Because I knit them myself for my..."

Peter's brow rose and his interest was piqued. "For your..."

"No one. For the soldiers."

"Am I not a soldier, Miss Murphy?"

"Well, yes, but —"

"Besides, a large shipment just arrived, which is why I took the two last pairs." Peter lifted one of the socks up. "And by the way, might I say that your knitting abilities are beyond what I would've expected of a well-to-do American girl."

The girl kept silent, but her eyebrows retained their scowl.

"Look, Miss Murphy, if you'd rather I put these socks back and instead take the socks that just arrived, I shall do so. Honestly, these are exactly the kind of socks I prefer, and in my favourite colours. And beautifully knit...." He looked down at her hands. "...by beautiful hands."

Her pale skin now blushing, the girl finally opened her mouth to speak. "It — it — well, it doesn't matter. You need them; you're a soldier, and I would like you to have them. I — I apologize, Major."

"Very well, then. Thank you, Miss Julia Murphy. I shall put these socks to good use."

The girl forced a smile. Peter couldn't stop staring at her. She was a lovely young woman, and he would be grateful for her gift, despite the initial begrudging nature of it. Her behaviour likely had something to do with his treatment of her a few weeks ago. Peter had been too cross with her, even under the circumstances.

In his motorcar on the way back to the office in Soissons, he found himself smiling at the girl's bold manner and her misunderstanding. Their banter back and forth had been most entertaining. She seemed very possessive about the socks she had donated. For whom had she initially knit them? In the end, she agreed that he could keep them. It was all strange and peculiar, but her feistiness — and her kindness — warmed his heart. He focused on the road ahead.

***

Instead of showing the major she wasn't going to be bullied, Julia wound up making a fool of herself. It would've been different had she not known who had received the socks. Now that she did, she felt a sliver of regret that she had given away one of her treasured gifts to

59

someone who was so obviously *not* her beloved.

Julia returned to the dormitory to answer her brother's letter. She tried not to give Major Winslow a second thought.

Chapter 8
A Dangerous Enemy

The month of April had turned into a soggy one with rain for two weeks straight. The constant downpour of the past two days put Julia on edge. There were three different holes in this barrack's roof and each time one was repaired, another would begin to drip.

The recent German offensive meant more casualties, and if Julia thought that she would eventually become accustomed to the soldiers' burns and gaping wounds, or their screams and moans, she was sadly mistaken. Instead, each day proved more difficult than the previous.

A few of the more experienced medical aid workers began organizing the wounded. They devoted one barrack to burn cases, one to influenza and another to those with fractures and lost limbs. And one barrack was set aside for the most critical cases. Of course, now there was also a death ward, for terminally ill soldiers.

Ann spent most of her time in the fractures and lost limbs ward. Charlotte now worked in the critical barrack. Julia spent some of her time in the burn ward — which she despised — but she preferred it to the death ward. Unlike some of her co-workers, she was not very good at pretending as if these men would get better. Some of the men in the death ward realized where they were; others did not.

Julia had the most sympathy for those conscious and rational soldiers. There was still so much life left in these young men that sometimes Julia couldn't bear to make eye contact. She shook her head at the sheer waste of life this war caused.

As the first week of May ended, influenza cases increased to the point where these patients were now taking up two barracks. Since when was the flu a problem in late spring? Julia hoped — and prayed — that she and the other girls would not contract this awful sickness. Men were developing fevers as high as 106 degrees. The stench of vomit and diarrhea hung in the air. A few of the infected soldiers had already passed away from pneumonia. Sister Agnes had asked for volunteers to work in the influenza barracks. Many girls had volunteered and Julia felt guilty for not doing so. But she had seen what this disease was doing to the bodies of young and vibrant men.

Several days later, some of the girls came down with fevers, became lethargic and began vomiting. Uninfected girls started wearing face masks to avoid catching the flu, but by the end of the following week, many of the soldiers and aid workers had contracted the deadly virus. Julia suspected that she would also become infected, but she hadn't yet. The situation was reminiscent of the time on the boat when everyone else seemed to get sea sick. Julia was thankful, but with so few healthy workers, she was often doing the work of four girls. Given the alternative — possible death — Julia was grateful. She saw not one, but two, of her fellow aid workers die from influenza in the ensuing week: young, vibrant girls like herself. And over 30 soldiers with minor wounds had already succumbed to the disease.

Within ten days, most of the girls and soldiers were recovering. Julia was thankful that the worst seemed to be behind them.

She had just finished working a long day without much to eat. Stopping by the dining hall, she picked up a small bowl of lukewarm vegetable stew, although it was more like soup. Julia ate quickly and hurried to her dormitory.

After removing her uniform and apron, Julia collapsed on her bed in her slip without reciting her usual prayers. An hour or so later, she woke up, lips tingling and nausea overwhelming her. She reached for a linen towel and doubled over. She vomited the stew she had eaten.

"Uh-oh, Jules. Let's hope you don't have influenza," she heard Ann's faraway voice say.

A few hours later, she was certain that she was dying. It felt like every bone and muscle in her body hurt and even her hair and teeth were sore. She moaned and heard Ann's voice through a fog of unconsciousness. "Jules, here is a pan for vomit and a glass of water, if you need it." Then she said something else, but all Julia heard was gibberish. Had someone driven a metal stake through her head? She had had headaches before, but had never experienced such an intense pain. And she was cold, so cold. No matter how many blankets covered her, she shivered, her teeth chattering until she thought they might break. *Death would be a welcome gift.* A few minutes of sleep here and there had not been enough to safeguard her from contracting the virus, especially since Julia's body was already so fatigued from long workdays.

By the third day, Julia was able to sit up for a brief moment. Her dreadful headache was nearly gone, and with it, every ounce of energy. She was too weak to eat and by the fifth day, Julia, already thin, just wanted to sleep.

Ann's soothing voice came to her ears. "Come on, Jules, you've got to try to stay awake and sip water. You're becoming dehydrated. You can do this." *Please let me sleep. I just want to sleep.* Ann's voice seemed distant as she urged her to sip. Too weak to protest, she obeyed.

The fever finally broke two days later, and Julia could sit up for longer periods. Now she understood why people were dying from this dreaded illness. It was the worst sickness she had ever had. For days, she was still so weak that she could barely get out of bed, but her friend Ann kept forcing her to walk, and Charlotte visited and offered to play her violin, to which Julia shook her head.

It took ten days of recuperation before Julia was able to work again. Sister Betty had told her that she would be with the men in the death ward, reading to some and writing letters for others because it would be less exhausting, and she could sit while doing so.

It may have been less tiresome physically, but more so emotionally. Julia wrote letters for four soldiers and read letters to five others. The most heart-wrenching was for a soldier named Sergeant Walter P. Gillespie, whose body was covered in large yellow blisters from mustard gas, and whose eyes were permanently blinded and seared shut. The poor man moaned and struggled with each breath as he told Julia what to write in a letter to his wife, pausing as he gathered the strength to say each word. *Dearest Trudie, I want you to know how much I love you and how much I don't want to leave you and the boys. The docs here say I have only a few days at best. When I'm gone, make sure to tell Walt Jr, Charlie and Jack that I love them too. Tell Walt he's going to be the man of the house now. Tell them to play sports and to treat girls with respect and kindness. Don't worry about me. I'm going to a much better place, a place without pain and suffering. God bless. All my love, Walt.* Julia kept blinking and pursing her lips to keep from crying. But her stuttering voice betrayed her tears. "Anything else, Sergeant?"

The soldier squeezed his eyes in pain as he tried to take a breath. He shook his head.

"I'll send this immediately, Sergeant."

Later that day, Julia was reading to another soldier when she glanced at Sergeant Gillespie's bed and saw a nurse pulling a sheet over his face. She sighed. *Requiescat in pace.* The poor man was no longer in pain.

On the weekend, Sister Betty told Julia that she could return to her job of preparing men for the operating theater. As tired as she still felt, she was thankful. Julia preferred to give care to unconscious men because she hated causing more pain to those who were awake. And their eyes. Julia could never forget the look in most of these men's eyes: fear, pain, sorrow, regret. In these boys, Julia could see the young men she knew: men from her parish, Ann's beau, her cousins. Thoughts wandered to her beloved and she scoffed.

Her beloved. She hadn't much time to think about her future husband most days, given the weakness and exhaustion she felt since being ill.

Julia frowned. Did her beloved even exist? Had she been too foolish, childish? Had her head been too high in the clouds?

She studied the unconscious man she was preparing for surgery. Blood and puss filled an eight-inch-long wound on his right leg. Burns covered his torso.

Julia shook her head, putting life in perspective. It was time she took her head out of the clouds and return to earth. This was reality. This was war. And maybe she was not meant to marry at all.

That evening, after a long day preparing men for surgery, she fell into bed. As she drifted off to sleep, she heard the hum of planes overhead. Julia recognized that German planes had a different sound, several tones deeper than the Allied planes.

The rattle of rapid-fire artillery sounded in the distance and grew louder.

Her eyes flew open as she realized that their field hospital was being bombarded with military fire. Did the enemy not see the huge red cross on the roof? She sat up in bed. In the darkness, she could see Ann, Charlotte and the other girls sitting up, waiting for the shooting to end. Ten long minutes later, it finally ceased and Julia and the others lay back in their beds.

No incoming wounded arrived for three days straight. In fact, the busiest barracks in recent weeks were the influenza tents. Just when Julia thought influenza cases were decreasing, 30 more men contracted the flu. It didn't seem to matter that flu cases were being quarantined and that everyone was wearing face masks or washing their hands and all surfaces. Men — and women — were still getting sick and some were dying.

Chapter 9
A Blood Red Sky

The middle of May brought brighter and sunnier weather. After an uneventful day working in the barracks preparing men for the operating theater, Julia slept better than she had in a long while. She had been dreaming about being home in Philadelphia with her family when a loud explosion woke her.

Ears ringing, she jumped out of her cot, pulled on her robe and followed Ann and the others. When they looked out the window, there was a collective gasp among the girls. Against the blood red sky of the dawn stood the large oak tree whose branches had spread over what used to be Barrack #49. The building had disappeared and, in its place, barren branches had blossomed with fragments of bodies, bits of bedding, furniture and hospital equipment.

Julia stared, unable to take her eyes from the scene. Since recuperating from the flu, she had not worked in #49, one of the influenza barracks. Many soldiers and some volunteers had just died a violent death. *Requiescant in pace.* Her eyes glistened as she fought back a sob.

"Those men were well enough to be moved to another barrack tomorrow." Ann's voice cracked.

"Yes." Instead their families would receive the awful news that their sons, husbands and brothers were now dead, not to mention the medical aid workers who had been there.

Looking around in the dorm, the red sky had lit up the room in a gory hue, a reminder of death. Julia couldn't see

Charlotte anywhere and her bed was untouched. "Where is Charlotte?"

"I don't know, Jules," Ann scanned the room. "She should've been in bed. She worked all day yesterday."

Julia tensed. *Please, God, let Charlotte be all right.*

The girls quickly dressed and raced to the barracks and to the scene of the explosion to ascertain whether they could help. When she and Ann arrived outside, Sister Betty called them over. "Ann, I need you at the scene of the bombing to recover bodies. Please wear a mask. Sister Margaret is in charge." She turned to Julia. "Go to Barrack 43. There's a Hun officer who needs attention. Major Winslow will be coming to interrogate this morning. There will be a motorcar arriving in a few hours to take him to the prisoners' camp. Ensure he is cleaned and ready to leave after Major Winslow speaks to him."

"Yes, Sister," Julia replied.

She stood in front of Barrack 43, but her attention was drawn to the devastation a few hundred feet away. The barracks on either side of Barrack 49 had been damaged and soldiers and nurses were injured. Just then, she saw Charlotte, holding a bandage to her head scarf which had turned red. But she was alive! "Charlotte!"

The girl turned and smiled as Julia ran to greet her. "I was so afraid that you were in the barrack that exploded."

"I was in the critical care unit beside it. Got a pretty nasty cut on my head. I'm happy to be alive."

"Thank God for that."

"Indeed. Thank God."

"Do you need help getting to the doctor? You're

bleeding quite a bit. I can take you there."

"No, I should be fine." She pressed the bandage onto her head. "I can get there on my own. Besides, I'm sure you're needed elsewhere."

Julia rubbed her friend's shoulders, then proceeded to her assigned barrack.

Once inside, Julia asked the nurse in charge where the enemy officer was. She was directed to the back corner where a handsome, blond man with blue eyes was sitting up in bed, staring in her direction. She never liked dealing with conscious Germans ever since Kapitän Reiniger had killed himself.

As she approached, she felt his eyes on her. "Miss, you are here to help me, yes?"

Surprised at his nearly flawless English, she nodded. "The major will arrive soon to interrogate you." She pulled the curtain around his cot, wondering why this particular enemy soldier was provided with a privacy curtain when no one else in the barrack had one.

The man smirked. "Ah, then I should look my best. I do need a shave, if you would be so kind?"

Julia shook her head. She would not fall for another ruse like that. "No, sir. If you want a shave, one of the others can give you a shave with your hands restrained."

He seemed unaffected by her comments. "Permit me to introduce myself. I am Dur — Major — Schmidt, Gerhard is my given name. And you are?"

Julia was warned not to fraternize with the enemy soldiers, but this man seemed so pleasant and welcoming. "Miss Murphy."

"Ah, Miss Murphy, you are very pretty."

Ignoring the comment, she picked up his chart at the foot of his bed and learned that he had a long and deep laceration on his leg that had become infected and was not healing. "Now, let's take a look at your wound and see if there are any further signs of infection." She lifted the sheet and gently pulled the bandage off. There was redness on the wound and a small amount of fluid. She cleaned it and applied a clean bandage.

"Aren't you interested in knowing how I learned to speak English?"

Julia tried to ignore him, but he kept saying, "Eh? Do you know?"

She turned. "Very well. How did you learn to speak English?"

"I was born in Deutschland but lived in Canada for many years. I also speak French."

Julia did not know how to respond, so she remained silent.

***

On the way to the field hospital, Peter reflected on the letter he had received earlier that morning. He and Smythe were being transferred soon, but the letter didn't specify when or where.

Both sides of the war had spies who worked for the other side. The German officer he would be "interrogating" was actually a spy for the Allies. Dur Schmidt had been born and raised in Kingston, Ontario. One year before the war, his family had moved back to Germany only to find he was expected to fight for the Fatherland. He did eventually enlist, but not before he contacted the Brits to volunteer as a spy for the Allies. He had told Peter that although he was German, he really felt Canadian. Like Peter, he also spoke multiple languages. Peter had been in contact with him one way or another for the past two years. Because of his university education, Dur Schmidt was given a commission early on. If the Germans discovered that Dur Schmidt was working for the Allies, he would be shot or hanged immediately. No one — except for Peter and one other person — knew of his active participation in assisting the Allies.

Peter arrived at the field hospital and jerked his motorcar to a stop. His mouth fell open and his stomach twisted. One of the barracks was obliterated. Another barrack was damaged. The damned Huns didn't care about the rules of war. They dropped a bomb on a hospital, killing the wounded and innocent nurses who cared for them.

For a moment, he tensed. He couldn't help but think of the feisty and pretty American nurse, Miss Julia Murphy. He hoped that she hadn't been a casualty.

Sister Betty, her expression grim, met him at his motorcar. "This happened half an hour ago." She shook her head and released a mournful sigh. "Every man and nurse in Barrack 49 was killed. Some were injured in the adjoining barracks." She paused. "The German officer you came to see is in 43. Go to the back, you'll see him."

Peter bowed his head in remembrance of the dead. "Any...nurses... killed?"

"Yes, two girls..."

Peter lowered his head.

"Two of our American girls."

His heart stopped.

"Such a shame, Major. But the whole war is a travesty. It's time for it to be over."

Peter nodded. "Yes, I do hope it soon ends." As he walked toward Barrack 43, he felt immensely sad. Had Miss Murphy been killed? Why hadn't he just asked Sister Betty? No, she couldn't have been killed. The statistics were in her favor. *Yes, she's all right.* He was sure of it.

Inside the barrack, Peter made his way to the back. Patients and workers were talking about the explosion and it took more effort to get to the back of the barrack.

He gasped in relief when he saw Miss Murphy. She was just pulling the curtain around a soldier's cot. Why did he feel such strong relief?

He caught her eye and she smiled.

"Miss Murphy," he said as kindly — and calmly — as he could muster. "Good morning. I'm...very sorry to hear about the loss of your fellow aid workers."

The girl nodded. "Thank you, Major. Dur Schmidt is ready for you behind this curtain."

"Excellent. Thank you."

Peter glanced at the other convalescing soldiers and determined there were no other Germans in this ward. He pulled the curtain back around and sat on a chair next to Dur Gerhard Schmidt. The conversation would take place as quietly as possible and in German rather than English, despite the fact that the man could speak flawless English and French.

In hushed German, Peter asked, "What can you tell me about the next offensive?"

Dur Schmidt whispered, in German, "The Huns are planning an attack on the Allies in Central France, with the goal of preventing further reinforcements from reaching British positions in the north."

Peter lifted up the sheet and looked at the size of the wound. In German, he said, "Nasty. How did you get it?"

"Shrapnel."

"Take it easy. We need you back on the battlefield." He paused, scanning the medical notes on Schmidt's chart. "It looks like you'll be having a bit of a holiday in Le Tréport. Your contact there is Major Collins. He's a doctor at the British-run hospital."

"How long will I be there before I'm transferred to the POW camp?"

"You're supposed to be there at least two days, so you'll have to escape before then. That particular hospital is run more like a hotel, and they're not very stringent about enemy soldiers."

"Good."

He nodded to Schmidt, pulled back the curtain, then began to make his way out of the building.

***

As Julia cleaned bandages at the back of the barrack, she heard the conversation going on with the German officer. The man spoke excellent English. Why was Major Winslow speaking in German with him? Perhaps he wasn't aware. She must inform Major Winslow that this enemy officer knew English.

Julia glanced back to see Major Winslow opening the curtain around the cot. She stood and dried her hands on a towel. "Major Winslow, may I speak with you?"

"Of course," he said.

Major Winslow had a very kind face, when he wasn't scowling, that is. His dark hair had the slightest bit of a curl.

She motioned for him to follow her to the back door of the barrack. The major opened the door and held it for Julia as she walked through. He followed.

Julia turned to face him, her hands on her hips. "Major, that enemy officer speaks flawless English."

"Yes, I know." The man seemed unaffected by her information.

Julia felt her face flush from her neck to her cheeks. "Of course, you would know. I just thought..."

"Not to worry. When speaking with an enemy officer, it's always better to do so in their native tongue. Good day, Miss Murphy."

"Good day, Major." Julia turned to open the back door of the barrack when she heard Major Winslow calling her name.

***

Peter was about to leave the barrack when, from the farthest recesses of his mind, he remembered Dr. K's suggestion that he find a friend to write to. Miss Murphy wasn't exactly a friend, but she could be engaging, feisty and was quite pretty. Before he thought any more about it, he returned to the area at the back of the barrack and called her name. "Miss Murphy?"

"Yes?"

"I wonder if you might...well...if you might be..."

"Yes?"

Avoiding eye contact, he continued stumbling his way through his question.

"I'm being transferred soon. I wonder...well, if I might have your permission to write to you from time to time?"

He finally made eye contact. The poor girl's face flushed a shade of crimson.

"Uh...I...well..." Her dark eyes now avoided meeting his. Was she going to refuse him?

The girl gave a shy tilt of her head, then finally responded. "Yes, Major. You may write to me."

"Thank you, Miss Julia Murphy." He lifted his pant leg to show her the familiar blue-green socks she had knitted.

She nodded. "You're quite welcome."

On his way back to his car, Peter felt thankful and a bit giddy. The fact that she had responded in the affirmative surprised him. He wouldn't allow himself to hope for anything other than a cordial correspondence with a volunteer.

***

That evening, Julia found herself more than a bit astonished at the major's desire to write to her. She didn't even know his first name. Of course, he wasn't asking if he could be her beau, just a friendly correspondent. Some of the other girls had started writing to previously injured soldiers who were back on the battlefields. According to the girls, the soldiers were very grateful for the mail.

Julia supposed that if she could make this Allied soldier's difficult life more cheery, it was the least she could do.

Chapter 10
On the Move

May 31, 1918

Peter placed the transfer orders on his desk. He and Corporal Smythe would soon be leaving Soissons and travelling to Paris. Soissons, despite its proximity to the front, was a quaint city and the people were not only resilient, they were kind and generous, especially to him and Smythe. But he would miss Madame Delacroix's flaky croissants.

Things were definitely looking up for the Allies. As much as Peter hated to admit it, the Americans were doing an excellent job. Most of his fellow Allies — Canadian, French, British and Australian — were exhausted physically and mentally. If this "war to end all wars" did end soon, the Americans ought to get credit where it was due.

He began packing up his belongings. His hands on the wool socks, he thought of Miss Julia Murphy. He would write to her when he arrived at his new quarters.

***

No new casualties meant a day of calm in fighting and shared time off. Julia, Ann and Charlotte had a chance to enjoy a picnic lunch of cold meat and weak lemonade under the maple tree near the *château*.

Instead of rushing about, most of the volunteers were enjoying the warm day by strolling the grounds of the field hospital. Volunteers wore their uniforms even on days off in case there were incoming casualties. Besides, the girls only brought one change of civilian clothes with them, which they wore when they visited the town.

Ann sipped her drink and leaned close to Julia. "Jules, do you ever wonder if your beloved is here in France?"

"I don't think much about my beloved anymore, Ann. Perhaps I'm meant to be a spinster."

"Oh, posh. You still have all those gifts, right?"

"Well..."

"What gifts?" Charlotte leaned in closer to Julia.

"Oh, just a fanciful notion I had back when I was a naïve child dreaming of a knight in shining armor."

"Do tell!" Charlotte's eyes were wide.

Ann spoke up. "Jules has bought or made a Christmas gift for her future husband every year for the past four years. The first year was socks, right?"

"Yes."

"How romantic, Julia, and how absolutely beautiful!" Charlotte had a smile so wide that Julia thought her face might burst.

"I'm not sure about that. Don't you think it's foolish?"

"Of course not!" Charlotte shook her head. "It's lovely."

"Don't let go of your dream, Jules."

"I may already have. I donated the socks to the soldiers." Julia kept quiet about who was actually in possession of the socks. She sipped from her glass of lemonade.

"What a lovely gift to the soldiers, Julia."

Ann touched her shoulder. "You can knit your beloved another pair..." She stopped, her eyes widening. "Wait. What if...what if the man who is destined to be your beloved actually received the socks?"

Julia sprayed out a mouthful of lemonade. "What?"

"What if..." Ann seemed to pause for effect. "...by some fabulous twist of fate, your socks actually ended up with your beloved?"

"That's ridiculous. He's just a soldier in need of socks and..."

"And what?" Ann leaned close.

"Nothing."

"Well, it sounds *very* romantic." Charlotte placed a hand on her chest and sighed. "Love found in time of war."

"It's not love, Charlotte."

"You never know. Maybe love is in the place you least expect it."

Julia shrugged her shoulders. She wouldn't tell the girls — not yet — that not only was Major Winslow wearing her socks, but he had also asked to correspond with her.

Chapter Eleven
Letter of Gratitude

June 30th, 1918

After leaving Soissons, Peter and Corporal Smythe had been ordered to proceed to Paris, where Peter spent most of his time in the translation department at the main Allied headquarters.

Peter hoped that Miss Murphy had remained at the field hospital near Soissons. He thought of her often, but hadn't a moment to write her a letter.

New orders arrived for Peter and Corporal Smythe: they were called to report to the front near Amiens in a few weeks. He had no idea how long he would be in that location. But he had an unusually free afternoon, so Peter sat down to write three letters. First, he wrote to his Mum Dad and Dot. Second, he wrote another one to his kid sister, Maggie. The third letter would be to Miss Julia Murphy.

My Dear Miss Murphy,

Thank you for your openness to receiving correspondence from me. It has been well over a month and I've been wanting to write to you for weeks, but have not had much time for correspondence.

It is with deep gratitude that I pen this letter to you. I wanted to again thank you for the finely made knitted socks. I realize that you did not expect that I would be the one who would receive these socks, but I'm truly thankful for them.

I do hope that you and your fellow aid workers are keeping as well as you can amidst the circumstances. When you write, please use the general address on the back of the envelope as I will be transferred yet again in a few weeks.

Very truly yours,

Major Peter Winslow

On the envelope, he wrote, *Miss Julia Murphy, c/o Soissons Field Hospital.* On the back of the envelope, he wrote, *Major Peter Winslow, Canadian Expeditionary Force, France.* He would try to write to Julia again before he settled in his new quarters.

***

July 10th, 1918

Two days passed without any new wounded, so Julia tried to relish whatever quiet days she was fortunate to have. In these times, she found herself thankful that her family wrote to her often. Every line she read transported her back home to Philly. Last week, she received a letter from her mother and her brother Jack again. He seemed to devour any information she could send about the war. But as her supervisor told her, she couldn't say anything too negative or too detailed, or it would be censored.

Julia hadn't seen much of Charlotte since her friend had started working in the death ward last month. Whereas Julia merely tolerated it, Charlotte seemed to embrace the responsibility of caring for men who had severe wounds and were near death.

Julia sat on a windowsill, gazing up at puffy white clouds that drifted lazily in the blue sky. Lush trees surrounded the *château* and tent barracks, making everything so picturesque. If one didn't know better, one might even doubt that a war went on nearby.

She descended the stairs to the first-floor foyer and strolled to the dining area for breakfast. She had just joined Ann when she heard the orderly yell, "Courier, mail, post!"

Since Julia had received two letters last week, she wasn't expecting any this week. However, she gravitated toward the young orderly until she, Ann and several other girls surrounded the man. He handed a letter to two of the girls, then held one out for her. "This one is for you, Mam'selle."

"Thank you. *Merci*." Turning the letter over, she saw that the sender was a Major Peter Winslow. She drew in a breath. *So that's his first name.* She quickly opened it and read.

"Letter from home, Jules?" Ann asked, looking over Julia's shoulder.

Trying to read the letter, Julia shook her head. "From Major Winslow."

"*The* Major Winslow?"

Julia scowled at her friend. "Yes, *the* Major Winslow."

"Why is *he* writing to you?"

Julia scoffed. "Last month he asked if he could write to me."

"What? And you kept that intriguing information from your dearest friend in all the world?"

"I didn't keep it from you, Ann. I just didn't think it was that important." Julia was surprised at Ann's reaction. Wasn't this just casual correspondence? Helping the morale of a soldier? Besides, it had taken weeks before Julia had actually received a letter.

"A man asks if he can write to you and you don't think to tell your best friend?"

"I just..."

Ann nodded. "Well, well, well. This is an interesting turn of events."

"It is not an interesting turn of events. I'm just a correspondent. Nothing more." She waved her hand.

"Mark my words, Julia. The major likes you. Why else would he ask to write to you?"

Shrugging her shoulders, Julia shoved the letter in her apron pocket.

Chapter 12
Evacuation

July 17, 1918

When Julia proceeded to prepare the next man, this German soldier's extra *accoutrements* indicated that he was an officer, and that likely meant that an Allied interrogator would soon be here. There seemed to be a different man each time and, oddly, she found herself missing Major Winslow.

She did her job quickly and the officer, who was quite pale and thankfully unconscious, was prepared for surgery. The poor man had a long, deep laceration down his right side. It looked like his kidney or some other organ was partially exposed. A yellowish fluid seeped from his wound, large yellow blisters covered his chest and both arms. She cleaned him as best she could and wrapped him in a sheet, reciting a prayer for him.

Sister Betty shouted, "Attention, everyone! The Germans have invaded Soissons and they are rapidly approaching. We need to evacuate. Immediately!"

Julia made a sweeping gaze of the barrack. What did it mean to evacuate? What about all the wounded? And weren't some men still in the operating theater?

The barrack became a flurry of movement with the volunteers and nurses rushing about. Julia glanced at Ann, both girls remaining where they were at a patient's bedside.

Looking in Julia's direction, Sister Betty shouted, "Move it! Gather your things as quickly as possible. We'll be traveling west towards Reims. When and if the Allies push the front back, we'll be able to return. Don't leave anything of value."

Julia and Ann rushed out the barrack, across the lawn to the *château* and upstairs to their third-floor sleeping area. Pulling open her nightstand drawer, she retrieved the small wooden box with the items she kept for her beloved as well as the letters she had received from home. Clothing and other personal effects meant nothing to her. As they were leaving, Julia turned to Ann. "Where is Charlotte?"

"I don't know, Jules. In the death ward, perhaps."

"But she must get her things and come with us."

"All right. Let's find her."

Julia and Ann passed workers placing the stable wounded into trucks. The girls learned that some soldiers were so ill that they wouldn't be moved from the field hospital. Instead, they were to be taken to the *château* where they would be gathered in one room. *Who would stay with these poor souls?* As if in answer to her thought, Sister Betty announced that Dr. K and Charlotte had volunteered to stay behind to care for the wounded.

No, it couldn't be! Charlotte had volunteered? Julia rushed to the *château* and followed two stretcher-bearers carrying a wounded man. Charlotte, her feisty friend, was assisting one man and holding a basin for a man who was vomiting.

Julia stared at her friend. "Charlotte, you're *staying*?"

The normally effervescent girl nodded. "I can't leave. I *want* to stay."

"But..."

"I'm staying, Julia. This is where I am meant to be."

"What can I do? Can I help you?"

"Actually, yes. I need paper to make notes. Perhaps a notepad or sheets of paper."

Julia turned to quickly discern where she could get paper. Then it dawned on her. She had a beautiful journal in the small box she carried. It was meant for her beloved, but Charlotte needed it now. She lifted the lid and showed her the small brown pocket journal. The girl glanced up.

"Where did you get this?"

"From a little shop in Philadelphia."

"Oh, no! Julia, this isn't meant for your beloved, is it?"

"It's fine, really. I can always buy another one."

Charlotte stepped back as stretcher-bearers took the wounded soldier down to the basement. She held the small book in her hands. "This is too beautiful to write in."

"I want you to have it. Please, Charlotte. Accept this gift from me."

Charlotte hugged her so tightly that she couldn't breathe. "I shall take good care of it."

"You can do whatever you'd like to it. It's yours now."

"Thank you so much, Julia. Godspeed."

"Godspeed to you, and to Dr. K and to all the men."

Dear God in heaven, keep Charlotte, Dr. K and all the soldiers safe from harm.

***

Five days later, with an American victory at Cantigny

pushing back the front, the nurses, volunteers and stable wounded were able to return to the field hospital. In her truck, they all sang *Yankee Doodle* — even the British, Canadian and French girls — and Julia had never been more proud of her fellow Americans.

When the *camion* arrived at the field hospital, the girls were still humming and giddy. Julia stepped out of the truck, a large pit forming in her stomach. Most of the barracks had been damaged or destroyed. Miraculously, the *château* containing all the critically injured along with Charlotte and Dr. Kilgallen received only minor damage. When Julia asked her friend what had happened, Charlotte lowered her head and bit her lip. "It's too much to go into now. I need sleep."

Julia's prayers had been answered, but there was much work to be done to rebuild and repair the barracks.

***

Only two days before he was scheduled to travel to Amiens, Peter found out that he would need to stop in Soissons on the way there. Since the field hospital was on the way to Soissons, he thought it would be an excellent chance to visit. He found himself unusually excited that he might have an opportunity to see Julia again. In the past few weeks, he couldn't stop thinking about her.

Here at the Allied office just outside of Paris, he could visit John's grave as often as he liked. Across the street, there was a small but thickly forested area with a natural path. Peter kept promising himself he would take a walk there but never had the time before today. Today would be the day.

Peter crossed the street and strolled a hundred feet in and came to a glade. The scent of summer flowers and rich soil calmed him. He sat down on the lush green grass and stared at the cerulean sky above. He tore the last two pages from his notepad. For the moment, the war was far away and this glade was as necessary as breathing. He began to write.

***

It was busy for the next few days. Julia and the other medical aid volunteers cared for the wounded in every space available in the *château*, the foyer, hallways, dining hall, even the basement room and kitchen.

Sister Betty had asked Julia and Thérèse to give hypodermics to the men lining the walls in the first-floor dining hall. Julia tried to engage Thérèse in conversation, but the girl only answered with one or two words. Upon studying Thérèse's face, Julia noticed the girl had a deep cut on her hand as well as a scrape on her neck.

"Thérèse, are you all right?"

She nodded but with pinched lips and eyes glistening. "But Sophie is not."

"Oh, no! What's wrong?"

"Our neighborhood was bombed during the recent attack. We didn't have time to get to the underground shelter. We were all in the basement and the house next door must have taken a direct hit that went through the roof. It destroyed most of our parlor; the furniture, the floor and everything else ended up in our basement. Miraculously, Mum, my daughter Sylvie, and I weren't injured except for cuts and bruises. But Sylvie's twin sister, Sophie, wasn't so lucky. I'm pretty sure she has a broken arm that needs resetting, as well as a deep gash in her leg that looks like it might be infected. I did my best to clean her wound and stitch it up but she's in tremendous pain. She needs to be X-rayed and have a cast applied."

"Have you brought her to St. Paul's in town?"

Thérèse nodded. "Unfortunately, a child with a broken arm and infected leg is low priority. They won't do anything until all the soldiers are treated. By that point, the arm will probably be permanently damaged."

Before she gave another soldier a hypodermic, Julia stood up and faced her friend. "Thérèse, I'm so sorry. What can I do?"

"My only option now is to take her to a Paris hospital. But the train fare alone will cost more money than I have, in addition to the hospital visit."

"How much would you need?"

"Not sure. The train fare would be about 150 francs roundtrip and I don't have that kind of money. I've been praying to the Blessed Mother and to my patron saint, Thérèse, the Little Flower, for a miracle."

Julia nodded.

They continued with their tasks, but Julia was already thinking of ways to raise money for Sophie. Maybe she could help Thérèse.

That night in the dorm room, Julia asked Ann, Charlotte and a few other girls if they had any prized possessions or money they could share or pawn to help Thérèse pay for Sophie's train ticket and medical expenses. A train ticket to Paris was expensive enough, but Thérèse would need more than that for lodging.

Julia's goal was to raise at least 250 francs. She had already decided to pawn the pocket watch. Yes, it was for her beloved. Besides, any material items could always be replaced. A child's health was at stake here.

The girls handed Julia about 40 francs. Not enough, but it was a start.

She'd have to wait for a lull in the fighting before she visited the pawn shop in Soissons, assuming there still *was* a pawn shop there, given the recent battle.

***

Two days passed with no new wounded. It was a sunny and warm summer's day, so Julia asked Ann if she'd like to travel with her into Soissons.

"Sure. Why?"

"I'm going to the pawn shop to hock the pocket watch."

Ann scowled.

"Don't scold me, Ann. It's for a good cause."

Her friend's expression softened. "I know. I hope the pawn shop survived. The man that runs it is so dear."

"Yes, he is. Shall we ask Charlotte to join us?"

"I don't think she will want to leave, Ann."

In the death ward, now the barrack closest to the *château*, Julia and Ann asked Charlotte if she'd like to accompany them to Soissons.

"No. Thank you for asking, though. Julia, I keep forgetting to tell you. I didn't actually use the lovely pocket journal you gave me because I found paper I could use."

Ann raised her eyebrows and leaned toward Julia. "What journal?"

Charlotte began talking with her hands. "Oh, here it is.

It's beautiful, with an embossed maple leaf on the front."

"My word! Jules, you gave away another one of your beloved's gifts?"

"Yes, I did, and it's hers now."

"When you pawn the pocket watch, you're not going to have any gifts left!"

"I'll have one: the Miraculous Medal. And that's fine with me."

"Are you sure you don't want this back, Julia?" Charlotte held the book in front of her. "I'm happy to give it back to you."

"No, no. It's yours. Please keep it – or give it to someone you think needs it."

Charlotte winked at her. "That's very kind of you."

***

Peter drove the motorcar towards Soissons, turning right at the intersection before the town and toward Vauxbuin. He was relieved to hear that, while the field hospital had taken artillery fire and many of the tents were damaged, no one had been killed.

"In case you're wondering, Smythe, I'm dropping something off at the field hospital." He didn't tell the corporal that he hoped he would see a pretty medical aid worker by the name of Miss Julia Murphy.

When they arrived, it seemed quieter than usual and less than half of the barracks were in place. Peter asked Smythe to remain in the vehicle while he went into the building and to the front desk in the foyer. However, there wasn't anyone at the front desk, so he stepped into the officers' ward only to find convalescing men smoking cigarettes.

In the closest barrack to the *château*, a sign indicated this was the "terminal ward." Peter opened the door and saw one of the aid workers, a dark-haired girl, sitting on the side of a cot and holding a soldier's hand. The girl hummed in a lovely, calm voice. Peter waited, listening. He didn't have the heart to interrupt her. This was the death ward and the girl was probably waiting for the soldier to die.

The girl finally stood, but not until after she made the sign of the cross and pulled the sheet over the man's face. Peter cleared his voice. When she turned and saw him, she offered him a wide smile. "Oh, hello! You're Major Winslow, aren't you?"

"Yes, I am. And you are?"

"Miss Charlotte Zielinski."

"Miss Zielinski, a pleasure to meet you. I was wondering if you might know where Miss Murphy is."

"She and another girl went into Soissons for the day."

Peter's shoulders sagged. "Is that right?"

"Yes."

"Well, I have a letter for her, if you wouldn't mind giving it to her."

"I'd be happy to do so." Miss Zielinski approached him and took the letter from Peter's hand. "I shall put it in my journal over here." She picked up a small brown journal and put the letter between the pages. Peter's eyes were drawn to the front of the small book.

"Beautiful. Is that a maple leaf on the cover?"

"Yes, I believe it is."

"The maple leaf is one of the symbols of Canada."

"Oh, I didn't realize that! Do you like this journal, Major?"

"It's quite nice and just the right size." He took out his own small pocket journal and held its frayed pages in front of her. "My journal has seen better days and there are no blank pages left. I'll have to buy another one."

The girl immediately straightened. "Wait! I haven't used this yet, Major. I would be happy to give it to you. Would you accept this gift from me?"

"Uh...no, no...I...uh...you should keep it. I can buy another."

"But I would like you to have it. Please. I don't really need it anymore and you are, after all, Canadian. You should have this journal with the maple leaf on it."

"Well, when you put it that way..." Peter held his hand out to receive the journal. He slid the letter from between the pages, handed it to her and accepted the journal. "You won't forget to give this to Miss Murphy?"

"I certainly won't, Major."

"Thank you, Miss Zielinski. You are very kind."

"You're welcome, sir."

Peter removed the other notepad, stuck it in his pants pocket and then slipped the new one in his breast pocket.

***

The barracks at the field hospital had taken so much

damage during the battle of Soissons that Julia expected to see worse destruction in town. However, when they arrived in downtown Soissons and stepped off the *camion*, Julia and Ann stood transfixed. The driver had to stop the truck at the edge of town since it appeared that most roads were not passable by vehicle. Rubble covered the streets and many homes were destroyed.

Julia said a quick prayer for all those killed and hurt during the last siege.

Next, the pawn shop. Despite the devastation, as they got closer to town, the streets were crowded with passersby and vendors selling fruits and vegetables.

"Look at this street, Jules. There are only a few buildings standing. It's awful."

"It is. Come, let's see if the pawn shop is still intact." They walked towards the pawn shop. As they ventured farther from the center of town, they noticed fewer people but more rubble as well as one dead horse in the road. *Thank God there are no bodies.*

Many houses were destroyed beyond repair, but Julia could still see portraits hanging on half-standing walls. She lowered her head and silently recited another prayer for all those who were killed, injured or homeless.

The girls climbed and stepped over piles of stone and wood here and there and finally arrived. Amazingly, the pawn shop was the only establishment on the street that was still in one piece. The front window was smashed, but the owner inside was speaking to a silver-haired woman.

The two girls entered and waited until the owner finished with his customer. Julia and Ann had met Monsieur Boulanger back in May when Ann had pawned a silk scarf so she could buy Theo a special gift. Monsieur was a short, middle-aged bald man with tiny glasses that he wore low on his nose. But he was kind and generous. Julia was surprised at how much he gave Ann for the scarf. This time, she hoped he would be just as generous.

The woman left and Monsieur Boulanger greeted the girls with a hearty, "Bonjour, Mam'selles!"

Julia exclaimed, "My gosh, your shop is the only one on the street still standing!"

"Oui, Mam'selle. My wife thinks it is a miracle. Not sure about zat, but I am very happy to still be doing business, especially with you lovely girls." Noticing the item in Julia's hand, he said, "You have more treasure for me to see?"

"Yes, Monsieur. It's a pocket watch, sterling silver, engraved."

He nodded and took it, looking at it through his little glasses, then shook his head. "But, Mam'selle, it's engraved. I'm afraid I cannot give you as much as if it weren't engraved."

Julia sighed. For the first time since buying the watch, she regretted having it engraved. "That's fine. What can you give me?"

"Well, what do you need zis for?"

"We're trying to raise money to help our friend's daughter. She needs to go by train to Paris to be treated by the physicians there. She was hurt in last week's battle."

"Oh, very sad. *D'accord.* I give you 120 francs. Does zat seem fair?"

Julia pursed her lips. 120 francs seemed fair, even

generous. "Yes, very fair, indeed. Thank you."

"Did you buy zis for someone?"

Julia and Ann exchanged glances.

"No – well, yes, I suppose I did."

"And you are selling it to give the money away?"

Julia nodded.

"I wish I could give you more, *ma chérie*, but I tell you what I do. I weel keep it here and save it for you in case you want to come back after the war and buy it back, yes?"

Julia smiled at his suggestion. "That's very kind of you, Monsieur, but we're in the middle of a war and you need the money too. This is yours now. I won't expect you to do that for me."

"Mam'selle, if you are selling it to me and it is mine, then I weel save it for you."

She wanted to hug the man. "*Merci, Monsieur.*"

"*De rien,* Mam'selle."

Julia added the 120 francs to the 40 francs the other girls donated. The two girls walked the five blocks to Avenue Château Thierry, where Thérèse and her family lived. Julia wished that she could've raised more, but 160 francs was an excellent start. At the very least, Thérèse could purchase the train tickets to Paris.

When they approached Thérèse's home, Julia could see that the glass in the front window was smashed. The houses on both sides were all-but-destroyed and in Thérèse's roof, a gaping crater. The door was open and they could hear voices inside.

Julia knocked. "*Bonjour*? Hello?"

A short, stocky woman in her 50's with salt and pepper hair and a black dress greeted them warmly. "*Bonjour.* Hello," she said with a British accent.

"Hello, ma'am. We're looking for Thérèse. I'm Julia Murphy and this is Ann Fremont.

"Oh, of course. Thérèse has told me about you both. I'm Emma, her mum. She's in the kitchen with Sophie. Come on in, and don't mind the mess. Step carefully." She pointed toward the parlor. "As you can see, our home is quite damaged, so the floor here may be unstable."

The two girls entered carefully. The scent of baking bread seemed out of place in the otherwise damaged house. To the right was likely what used to be the parlor, but it appeared as though a bomb had exploded outward from the floor, with only the front and side walls and part of the roof still intact. To the left was a staircase filled with bits of wallboard and wood. They followed the older woman through a narrow hallway, stepping over pieces of plaster, wood, roof tiles and other debris that were scattered on the floor. The wall to the right was speckled with bits of metal but still standing.

The entrance to a kitchen stood at the end of the hallway. Thérèse sat in an armchair and held onto a small dark-haired girl. The girl hid her face and wept quietly.

Thérèse looked up and gasped. "Julia! Ann! How wonderful to see you both. Please come in. Mum will make you some tea."

"Thank you." Julia glanced around the spacious kitchen, which seemed to have escaped damage, for the most part. Two mattresses lined the left wall, where the family was probably now sleeping. Cracked windows looked out onto a small yard. An identical dark-haired girl –Sylvie – was in the yard. She was throwing a ball high in the air and catching it. *The wonder of a child who can play amidst war.*

Julia and Ann sat down at the table. "Thérèse," said Julia, "we have something for you." Taking the bills and coins from her front pocket, Julia pushed them across the table to Thérèse.

"What is this, Julia?"

"I wish it were more, but this is to help you buy a train ticket to Paris for you and Sophie. It's from Ann and me, as well as some of the other medical aid workers."

Thérèse drew in a breath. "Mum, I told you that Our Blessed Mother and St. Thérèse wouldn't let us down. Now we have enough money! Thank you, Julia and Ann, and to the very generous volunteers!"

"You *do* have enough?"

"Yes, Mum pawned the last of her jewelry, and I pawned my wedding ring."

"Oh no, you had to pawn your wedding ring?"

"Monsieur Boulanger said that he would keep it for me. Isn't he a kind man?"

"He certainly is."

"And now there's enough for a return trip, lodging and hopefully enough to set Sophie's arm. Oh, dearest Julia and Ann, I cannot thank you enough for this wonderful gift!" Thérèse began to cry and laugh at the same time. She kissed the top of her daughter's head. "We're going to Paris, Sophie, and you'll feel better soon!"

Chapter Thirteen
Surprise Rescue

After leaving Thérèse's house, Julia and Ann made their way down *Avenue Château Thierry* to the *Saint-Gervais-et-Saint-Protais* Cathedral.

As they got closer, they could see damage to the top of the spire, but they didn't take in the full devastation to the beautiful gothic cathedral until they rounded the corner and arrived at the front of the building. They had heard from Thérèse that it had already suffered damage throughout the war with a hole in its roof, and with gaps in its side walls, but now? A third of the roof was no longer there. Looking at it from this angle, rubble from other buildings seemed to have been dumped on both sides, making entrance into the church nearly impossible from those doors.

However, most of the walls were still standing. Julia shook her head. One would think that religious buildings would be exempt from wartime destruction.

The two girls stood, gazing upward. Julia had been in France for four months and had yet to have the opportunity to step inside any church. Staring at the cracked walls of the majestic cathedral, Julia felt compelled to go inside. Despite the devastation, this was still sacred ground. She needed to pray.

"Come on, Ann. Let's go inside."

"What? Is it safe?"

"Not sure, but the structure is still standing, which is more than we can say for most of the buildings in Soissons.

Besides, we'll just say a prayer and leave."

Julia and Ann climbed the stairs. At the doors of the church, a sign had been posted: *"Danger: Entrez à votre propre risque."* Julia didn't speak or read French very well, but she was pretty sure the sign was warning people that it was dangerous to enter. Despite the danger, the cathedral seemed to beckon her to go inside. She opened the doors, and the two girls entered.

In front of the foyer just beyond the arch, a pile of debris filled the nave. They had to climb carefully over the rubble until they were inside – if one could call it "inside," given the large gaping hole above revealing blue sky. Farther ahead, the altar and choir area appeared to be less damaged. After they wandered through the nave, Julia faced the altar. She felt a breeze and shivered.

Julia turned toward the northern transept and stared. Despite the damage, this sacred building was still breathtaking. Like most medieval churches, it was built in a cross shape. Moving into the transept – or the transverse part of the cross structure – Julia studied the beautiful painting that hung high on the wall above an exterior door. She read aloud a plaque below the painting, "Adoration of the Shepherds, by Peter Paul Rubens."

"Beautiful," Ann whispered behind her.

"It is, isn't it?" Julia thanked God that this precious artifact had escaped damage.

Julia made the sign of the cross and began to pray for all the souls lost, for those who were wounded and for this beautiful cathedral to be rebuilt. She prayed for Thérèse's and Sophie's safety and that Sophie's injury would be healed. Most importantly, she prayed for the death and destruction to end.

In Soissons, Peter parked the motorcar and asked Smythe to stay with it. Rubble filled the roads. Given the devastation of the city, he feared that someone would steal the car, regardless of where he parked, if he left it alone.

As he strode toward the city's centre, he shook his head. The city must have taken many direct hits from artillery fire. Rubble and ruins filled the streets and sidewalks, but the streets were busy.

The building that previously served as his headquarters had taken so much damage that Peter wondered where the Allied officer stationed there had gone during the bombing. After asking passersby, Peter found out that the office's new headquarters were in another bank close by on Boulevard Jeanne d'Arc.

Peter dropped off the papers, then made his way toward Madame Delacroix's place to check on the elderly woman. She lived right next to the cathedral and as he inched closer to the church, he shook his head. Lifting his chin, he stared. *What a waste.* The cathedral was not totally demolished, but it had taken quite a beating. And yet it was still standing. Whoever built this church obviously knew how to construct a building to withstand destruction.

Staring at the cathedral made Peter think of his brother John and his strong faith. It seemed a coincidence that the name of the church where his brother died – *Saint-Gervais-et-Saint-Protais* – bore the same name as this cathedral here in Soissons.

The beautiful building also brought a flash of Julia's face to his mind, and he said a quiet prayer that she was safe.

A prayer that Julia would return his affection also passed through his heart, but that would be selfish. If it was meant to be, it would happen.

***

Julia had just finished her prayer when she felt an urgency to leave. She heard what sounded like a tank drive by and the ground below the massive building shook. "Come on, Ann, we need to leave." Suddenly, Julia heard a crashing sound and turned to see long beams of wood and debris falling onto the growing pile near the arch of the foyer. Dust particles swept through the air.

Julia gasped and held her hands over her mouth. Coughing, she turned to Ann. "I'm sorry I didn't take that sign more seriously. I should've known better. Forgive me."

"No need. I followed you inside, remember?"

The pile of debris and rubble near the foyer had grown higher and more perilous than before. As well, the dust from the debris became thick closer to the front. "There's a door right here, Jules. Let's try it and see if it will open."

Julia turned the handle and pushed. The door gave way a few inches before it stopped. Peering out, Julia saw that chunks of stone and rock blocked the doorway. She listened for voices. When she heard two women, Julia shouted to get their attention. Two middle-aged ladies and an elderly woman climbed over stones and rocks, making their way to the door. Unfortunately, they couldn't speak English, but they understood enough to know that the girls were stuck and couldn't open the door. An older man showed up, but even with all of them helping, they couldn't remove the large stones blocking the doorway.

***

Peter walked by the chapel extension to see a gathering of people speaking and shouting at a side exit door of the cathedral. He picked his way carefully over stones and rubble. As he got closer, he realized that one massive stone and several smaller rocks blocked the door. He recognized the very large Madame Delacroix waving her hands and trying to speak to – was someone in the cathedral? Madame, two other women and an older man were trying to move the stones, to no avail.

He joined the group. In French, he asked, "May I be of assistance?"

Madame answered in French, "Major, you are a sight for sore eyes." She squeezed him so hard he couldn't breathe.

He stepped away. *"Est-ce qu'il y à l'intérieur?"* *Is someone inside?*

She answered in French that two American girls are stuck behind the door, and they can't move the stones and rocks to free them.

Peter let them know that he would be happy to help. *"Ah, bien, Madame. Avec pleasure."*

He studied the largest stone and wondered how he might move it. The back end of an axe would likely break it in enough pieces to move it.

To the elderly man, he asked, *"Monsieur, avez-vous une hache?"*

"Oui, oui," he said and ran off.

"Hello, hello?" Peter heard the sound of a young woman's voice.

"Yes, I'm here. I'm an officer with the Canadian army, and I'm going to help you get out. Are you hurt?" He could only see a shadow of one and the arm of another.

"We're fine, a little frightened, but fine."

The young lady's voice sounded familiar. *No, it couldn't be.*

"What are your names?"

"My name's Julia and my friend's name is Ann."

Peter's mouth fell open. "Julia...Murphy?"

"Yes, yes, I'm Julia Murphy!"

"Julia, it's Peter – Major Winslow."

"Oh my word, Major! Thank God you're here! Are you able to move the debris in front of the door?"

"I've sent the gentleman to get an axe. It might take some work, but I'll get you out of there."

"Thank you so much."

"How did you get in?"

"The front doors. It looked safe enough at the time. Now there's a high debris pile preventing us from getting out that way. And we didn't want to take the chance since beams of wood have been dropping from the damaged roof."

"Ah. I see."

Madame was looking curiously at Peter so he indicated to her that he knew the girls. *"Je connais les femmes, Madame."*

"D'accord," she nodded.

The man returned with the axe. Peter asked the onlookers to stand back. The elderly man begged Peter not to break his axe and to make sure he used the back end. "*Oui. Je comprends, monsieur.*"

Once everyone moved away, Peter drew the axe back and swung. He hit the largest rock repeatedly before it cracked into several pieces. He did the same with the second largest stone until it cracked into several more pieces. The group cheered, then they helped him move the pieces away so that he was finally able to open wide the door.

***

Julia's hands trembled when she clasped onto Peter's as he assisted her outside. "I don't know how to thank you, Major."

"No need, really. I'm glad I was in the vicinity."

To the rest of the crowd, Julia said, "*Merci beaucoup.*" The ladies applauded and the older man gave them a wink. After all these people had been through – a recent battle in their city and the other battles that had taken place here – they were willing to come out and help complete strangers.

The elderly lady embraced Julia, then Ann. The woman said something to the others and they soon dispersed, but not until after she gave the major a very vigorous hug. *This woman is obviously one of Major Winslow's admirers.*

Peter cleared his throat, then leaned over to pat the dust from his pants. Julia studied him. She hadn't realized it before, but Major Peter Winslow was actually more than average-looking. He was quite handsome in a wholesome, boy-next-door way.

"Now, I would highly recommend staying out of

bombed-out churches for the near future." He cocked one eyebrow and grinned as he spoke.

"Yes. Have you returned to Soissons permanently?"

"No, just for the day. I left a letter for you at the field hospital with Miss Zielinski."

"I haven't had a chance to respond to your first letter."

"That's quite all right."

The three stood awkwardly, with Major Winslow smiling at her and with Julia clearing her throat and shifting from side to side.

Ann finally broke the silence. "Major Winslow, would you like to join us for a picnic lunch? We have enough food in our basket to share. It's the least that we can do to thank you for rescuing us from the cathedral."

With his wide eyes and smile, the man looked as if they had offered him gold or something more valuable. "Actually, I would very much like to accept your invitation, but my corporal is waiting and we are expected to arrive at our next posting before dark. I had to leave the motorcar a few blocks from here because most of the town roads are impassable. "

"Can we walk you back and bid goodbye to you there?" Ann asked.

"Of course."

As they strolled along rubble-filled streets and sidewalks, Julia surmised that Ann remained a few paces behind to give the two of them privacy to talk. However, it made Julia feel more awkward, and she kept pausing to walk with Ann.

"Jules, please don't worry about me. Walk with the major. I'm sorry to be so slow, but I'm studying everything around me so I can describe it properly in my next letter to Theo."

The major smiled, as if agreeing that it would be a good idea for the two to walk together. Julia gave in and awkwardly walked beside him. Her heart was still racing from the excitement at the cathedral.

Peter spoke first. "Where in the United States are you from?"

"Philadelphia."

"Your family must miss you."

"Yes, and I miss them as well. My brother Jack is nearly 17 and wants to enlist. He needs a knock over the head! He has no idea what war entails."

Peter chuckled, then lowered his gaze. "Sadly, I was all-too-enthusiastic about enlisting too."

Julia found herself wondering about the major's family. "And you? Your family must also miss you."

Peter nodded and kept his chin down. "Even more since my brother was killed."

"Yes, that's right. I'm so sorry for your loss."

"Thank you. John was the oldest and did just about everything better. He was a natural at sports. He was always kind and generous. John was also the more virtuous of the two of us. He never missed an opportunity to attend Mass or the sacraments, despite the war."

"That's beautiful."

"He was very devout." He paused. "I also have two younger sisters."

"That's swell. With three younger brothers, I have always longed for a younger sister. My brother Jimmy is eleven and Joey is seven."

"I rather enjoy having younger sisters. Dot is 21 and is rather quiet. Maggie is 16, but she's got the wit of a 30-year-old." They walked in silence for a block. Peter gazed off into the distance. Julia glanced back at Ann, who winked at her. Julia tried to scowl, but it ended up in a smile.

"Uh...where in Canada do you live?"

"About 45 miles west of Ottawa in a small logging town called Arnprior."

"I hate to admit this, but I don't know much about Canada or the geography."

"Well, I don't know much about the states either, though I do know that Ottawa is 100 miles north of the New York state border."

"Really? That close?"

"Yes."

"Do they speak French in your hometown?"

"Yes. In Arnprior, there's more English than French, but there are still a few francophones. My grandmother was French so our family is bilingual. But the town of Arnprior was actually founded by a Scotsman and named after Arnprior, Scotland."

"Interesting. And you also speak German?"

"Yes." He stopped walking and turned to face her. "Miss Murphy – Julia – I don't know when I'll get to see you again. May I continue writing to you?"

"Yes, I would like that very much."

Julia stopped for a moment to catch her breath.

"Are you all right?"

She nodded. "I think my heart is still trying to settle from the incident back at the cathedral."

"Ah."

As the group approached the car, the man inside got out. He was a slender chap with a kind face and dark eyes. He took off his cap.

"Corporal, this is Miss Julia Murphy and Miss..."

"Ann Fremont."

"Ann Fremont."

"Nice to meet you, ladies." The corporal got back into the car while the major turned toward the girls.

"Miss Fremont, it was a pleasure to meet you. Miss Murphy..."

"Please call me Julia."

"Julia." He reached out to shake her hand. "Please stay in touch."

"I will. Godspeed, Major."

"Peter."

Julia nodded. "Godspeed, Peter."

***

During the entire ride back to the field hospital, Ann pestered her about Major Winslow. "The way he looked at you, Jules. He's smitten. He is in love with you. And heck, if a man rescues you from a — "

"He rescued you, too."

"Yes, well, I already have a beau. I'm telling you. He likes — maybe even loves — you."

"I don't know about that, Ann."

"I'd stake my life on it. I bet that Major Winslow is your beloved."

"I...I'm not...I don't..."

As they were getting out of the truck, Charlotte met them. "Julia, I have a letter for you from Major Winslow."

"Major Winslow saved the day!" Ann clasped her fingers together and held them in front of her in dramatic fashion.

"What?"

"We got trapped in the cathedral and he rescued us!"

"Ann, we weren't really trapped. The door wouldn't open because of the debris in front of it and he helped, that's all."

Charlotte still held the letter in front of her. "It sounds wonderfully exciting."

"Jules, things happen for a reason. It's fate, I tell you."

Ignoring Ann, Julia turned toward Charlotte. "Thank you, Charlotte." Julia took the letter and opened it.

Dear Miss Murphy,

I hope this letter finds you well. Let me assure you that my intentions are quite honourable. First, this unfortunate soldier is thankful that you knit these socks, even if I wasn't your first choice of benefactor. And I must admit that you have left quite an impression on me. I hope you will accept this sonnet as gratitude for your kindness to me.

The Glade
by Major Peter Winslow
for Miss Julia Murphy

Through forest deep the way is ever fraught
With threat unseen and callings scarcely heard
O'er beds of root and 'neath the midnight bird
The torturous amble quells all clement thought.

Then glory's arms embrace the step that's made
From shadow to the clearing's edge at last
Where spans the reach of grass so calm and vast;
That generosity, that gift, the glade.

And so my young dear's heart gives rest to me
And other gifts, outpoured relentlessly,
Such that cold reason makes the impious plea
That this feign'd heav'n, this heart, could never be.
Yet sun in skies azure flood certainty
Until my eye believes, this love — I see.

I cannot say where I will be stationed for the next few weeks, but you will remain close to my heart.

With kindest regards,

Peter

She looked up from the letter. "Very well. I will admit that he likes me. That doesn't mean he's my beloved."

Charlotte's eyes widened. She opened her mouth to speak but kept silent.

"What?"

"Do you remember the journal you gave me before the evacuation, the one with the maple leaf on the cover?"

"Yes."

"You had originally bought it for your beloved, right?"

"Yes, but I gave it to you."

"And I gave it to Major Winslow."

For a moment, Julia couldn't speak. Peter now had the journal that was originally meant for her beloved. Finally, she stuttered, "Wh...what?"

"He seemed to like it a lot. Did you know that it has a maple leaf embossed on the cover?"

"I knew it had a leaf, yes."

"Well, it just seemed so right to give a journal with a maple leaf on it to a Canadian, who just so happened to need a pocket journal."

With hands on their hips, Ann and Charlotte stood in front of Julia. Ann was staring at her, eyebrows lifted, mouth pursed. "He's got one of the gifts for your beloved. Fate, I tell you."

Julia lowered her head, then lifted her chin to look at Ann. "Actually, he now has two."

"What?" they exclaimed in unison.

"He happened to get the socks I knit for my beloved after I donated them."

"That clinches it," said Ann. "What's in the letter?"

"I'd rather not share it yet."

Ann scoffed. "Very well. But mark my words, Jules, Major Winslow is your beloved."

Back upstairs, in the silence of the dormitory, Julia read the sonnet again. It was...well, beautiful. The richness of his words was mesmerizing. Major Winslow — Peter — had composed this beautiful sonnet. For a moment, the poem transported her far away from the war, and she drank in the rich language.

And so my young dear's heart gives rest to me
And other gifts, outpoured relentlessly,
Such that cold reason makes the impious plea
That this feign'd heav'n, this heart, could never be.
Yet sun in skies azure flood certainty
Until my eye believes, this love - I see.

Amidst the atrocities of war, this poem brought beauty to her soul. She closed her eyes. *Could Major Winslow be my beloved?*

Julia shook her head. Her beloved would never have been so cross. Yes, she realized it was because his brother died. Yes, the major apologized. Yes, the major could write lovely, rich-in-language, sonnets. Yes, the major seemed like a nice man, after all. Yes, he was handsome in a boy-next-door way. Yes, Major Winslow was an Allied soldier. But...but...*was* there a but?

***

Around dusk, Peter and Corporal Smythe arrived at the

Allied farmhouse near the banks of the Sommes between Amiens and Picquigny. The next morning, after setting up the wireless equipment, Peter and Smythe explored the property. It included a farmhouse, barn and an overgrown and ignored garden. The house had seen better days, and he was thankful it was summer because there were holes in the roof. Smythe would hopefully fix some of the holes before the next rain.

As he and Smythe surveyed the property, Peter decided to check out the barn. As he approached, the whine of an animal travelled from inside the barn. Opening wide the doors, he waited and listened again for the sound, his hand on his gun. If the animal had rabies, he might have to shoot it. He clicked his voice to get the attention of the animal, hoping it wasn't one that would attack. But then he heard the whine again and was sufficiently convinced that it sounded like a dog. Moving closer to the noise, he noticed an emaciated German shepherd or Lab mix and her weeks-old pups. The poor animal needed food as her pups probably weren't getting the nourishment they needed from her nursing. Leaning his head outside the barn, Peter called to Smythe. "Can you see if there's any canned milk in the house? Maybe some canned meat? I found a dog and her pups in here."

"Right away, sir."

Peter crouched next to the black-and-white long-haired dog and her two pups. She could barely move, likely from hunger, and yet she still had energy to wag her tail. He patted her head. The pups were alive, but lethargic.

When he stopped patting her head, the dog nudged his hand to continue the gesture. Peter smiled. "You like to flirt, eh? Very well, little Coquette. That's what I shall name you."

Smythe brought him an open can of meat and a tin of milk. Peter dumped the meat in front of Coquette. "I know what you're thinking, Smythe. That we shouldn't be giving our rations to a dog who's likely going to die."

"Actually, I wasn't, sir."

"Good. How well-supplied is the house?"

"Extremely well, sir. That's why I was easily able to find the can of meat."

They watched Coquette nearly inhale the food, then Peter allowed her to slurp the milk. The grateful dog wagged her tail. Once finished, Peter took each pup and forced a bit of milk in each mouth. Leaving the now-satiated animals in peace, Peter and Smythe left the barn and proceeded across the laneway to the house.

Their British comrades had prepared the farmhouse well with a bunker in the basement supplied with food, cots and wireless equipment in case the Huns returned and they needed to hide. Even though they were given directions for how to find the bunker, what gave Peter consolation was that it took 20 minutes to find the latch. They knew that the bunker was behind the bookcase, but they couldn't find the lever to open it. Finally, a latch clicked at the very top and toward the back, hidden in the shadows, and it opened into what looked like a closet. It was small, about seven feet by seven feet with one shelf of canned goods, flashlights, two narrow cots, equipment and a few rifles and water. A pipe going up through the wall and out through the roof of the farmhouse would bring in ventilation.

If they needed to use this place, they would have to take care in opening, then closing, the bookcase to keep the books in place.

The two men returned upstairs to the dining room. A calm in the fighting meant there was an increase in communications. He scanned the room until his eyes came upon the large bag of correspondence the corporal brought with them. Peter would be censoring the letters when he had a few free moments. His least favourite duty. It was an important one because morale had to be kept positive back home in Canada. If there were too many details from the front, he had to cross things out. If the soldiers inadvertently wrote about the cities or towns in which they were stationed, he also had to censor that. The letters from a soldier to his sweetheart were the most awkward to read, especially since he knew many of them would not be returning home.

Peter relaxed in the chair, took Maggie's last letter from his bag and began to read.

Dear Pete,

I hope this letter finds you safe and well. Mum is more worried about you since John's passing. She and Dad are finally starting to smile again, although it's still rare. The light seems to have gone from their eyes. I miss John dreadfully. I keep thinking of his peculiar way of laughing and the way you two would tease me when I was little. But John is gone, and he wouldn't want us to be sad all the time. Dot and Mum keep busy with their work for the war effort at the paper mill. Dad stays busy at the office. In fact, he's been spending a lot of time there. So...just a warning: don't you dare die, Pete. No matter what! Come back to us alive! For Mom and Dad's sakes. And for mine and Dot's!

The last time John wrote to us, he told us that he had met a girl named Laura. The only thing he told us was that she was a telephone operator. I keep thinking of her. Poor girl. Poor us, too.

Speaking of meeting women, I had this odd notion today that perhaps you would come home with a French or British wife. Please! If you are indeed carrying on a torrid affair with a foreigner, do tell!

Peter raised his head and the corner of his mouth lifted in a smile. Thinking about it, though, perhaps Maggie was not too far from the mark. Admittedly, he did like a foreigner, although he somehow never thought of Americans as foreigners, given that they were Canada's southern neighbour.

Miss Julia Murphy was even lovelier than he had remembered. And after seeing her in Soissons, Julia may have an idea that he had this — affection — towards her. Even after his initial wretched treatment of her, she had been agreeable to receiving his letters. And she'd seemed cordial — even happy — to see him.

***

For the past five days, Peter had worked around the clock translating intercepted messages on his wireless. He had no time to think about anything other than translations.

It was a tricky situation, and he spent a lot of time translating the ones that were obviously decoy messages meant to confuse the Allies. Some were genuine chatter about strategy. He translated each one, though, and sent them to the local field commander, making notes as to which ones he thought were decoy messages and which were true. If he was correct, the enemy had three different plans for pushing back the front. Translating was mind-exhausting work, made all the more challenging with the booming sounds of bombs and occasional planes overhead. On the Allied front, troops were being sent to Ypres to trick the enemy into believing the next offensive would be north to Flanders. In fact, from previous missives, Peter found out that the surprise attack would be close to where he and Corporal Smythe were currently staying.

With the exception of the basement bunker, the farmhouse still appeared uninhabited. This morning, he had gone out to the farmhouse and discovered that the two pups had died in the night. Coquette had wagged her tail when she saw him but wouldn't move. So Peter buried the pups, then brought her into the farmhouse with him. He placed some clothes on the floor, and Coquette settled in nicely, though her eyes seemed sad.

Now, to the outside world, the only indication there might be occupants on this property were the motorcar and bicycle, but they were kept inside the barn.

The biggest challenge at present were the flying insects, rats and mice that seemed to think they owned this place. Perhaps Coquette could help in that regard. After all, the pests made it impossible to sleep, but then again, he could only take quick catnaps here and there anyway. When he did drift off for a few moments, the image of Miss Murphy often floated through his dreams.

He sat up and took the headphones off. The creaking of the floorboards behind him prompted him to turn around. Corporal Smythe held an envelope out to him, as he did every third day around the same time.

"Sorry for the interruption, Major, but you've got a letter." Corporal Smythe handed it to Peter.

Smiling, he said, "Ah, maybe another letter from Maggie." Then he glanced at the return address. *Miss J. Murphy, c/o Field Hospital, Soissons, France.* His mouth fell open and his eyes widened.

"From your friend, Miss Julia."

"Thank you, Corporal."

His pulse quickening, Peter slid the letter from the envelope. A grin plastered to his face, he unfolded the letter and read.

Dear Major Winslow,

I must say that I was delighted to receive your second letter and I gratefully accept your beautiful sonnet, which I keep close to me at my bedside.

It was such a surprise to see you in Soissons. Thank you again for assisting us out of the cathedral.

I do pray that the war ends soon and that God watches over you and the corporal.

By the way, do you remember the journal that Charlotte gave you? Well, I had originally given it to her. When she told me that she had given it to you, I was very happy that you will be able to use it. I must admit that before the war, I did not know that the maple leaf was a symbol of Canada. But I agree with my friend, Charlotte, that it is a most appropriate journal for a Canadian (despite the fact that I bought it in Philadelphia!)

I was happy to learn about your family. Please tell me more about them and about Arnprior and Canada.

Have you ever traveled outside of North America

before? I had never been anywhere except Philadelphia and the Jersey shore until I set sail for Europe back in March. I would have preferred to see and enjoy France without the booming of guns, bombs, planes and artillery sounds.

I do hope the fighting is not dreadful where you are stationed. It has been quiet and very warm these past few days, and I do so enjoy taking pleasant strolls around the grounds.

Praying that Jesus, Mary and Joseph keep you safe.

Sincerely Yours,

Julia

Peter smiled the entire time he read the letter. She kept his sonnet close to her? And the journal that was in his breast pocket was originally Julia's? The small book now held more meaning for him, and he would treasure it, like the socks, for they were both — at least originally — from Julia.

Chapter 14
A Plea From Romeo

A week later, Ann burst through the door of the barrack where Julia was preparing soldiers for the operating theater. "You have a letter from your Romeo, Jules." She gave Julia an envelope.

Julia's eyebrows lifted. "*My* Romeo?"

"Look."

Another letter from Major Winslow.

Her heart started racing.

Ann's voice prompted Julia to look up. "I hope that Major Winslow is not in need of a pocket watch now that you've hocked it, Jules."

"That's not amusing." Opening it, she scanned his letter, but it would have to wait until she was finished in the ward. She stuck the letter into her pocket and finished her shift.

At the end of her shift, Julia grabbed a piece of bread in the dining hall and raced upstairs to her cot. She took out the letter and drank in the rich, beautiful words.

Ellen Gable

The Paladin Unmade
by Peter Winslow

'Tis such a man as walks the path forbade,
By those whose warnings tell of threats unthought,
'Tis such, invites the thunderous awe that's wrought
By He, from whom all thunderous things were made.

This man amused by coming storm or war,
Stands grounded though the stench of death surrounds.
Eyes heavenward where surely strength abounds;
Foot to soil, despite its stain of gore.

Then how, 'tis love that brings him to his knees,
Head to bow, and desperate plea for aid?
The hero left? The paladin unmade?
For one beloved nod, that she agrees,
The soldier and the knight desert their raid,
And pray that love for war be trade.

P. Winslow to J. Murphy

This sonnet is written only for you, but is dedicated to all the beaus who are courageous during battle but unassuming — and maybe even fearful — in the face of love.

Speaking of beaus, do you have one back home?

She shook her head, her eyes still staring at the letter. The sonnet, it was painfully beautiful. The major was clearly a wise — and lonely — man. Of course, the war made every person lonely.

But he uses the word beloved and love in his poem to me. And he asked if she had a beau.

How would she respond? No, she did not have a beau. She could say, "Well, yes, I do have a detailed image in my mind of who my beloved should be and have already bought gifts for him which I no longer have because I gave two of them away and you wound up with them and I hocked one to help an injured child." It all sounded absurd. No, she would not say that. The man would think her mad.

Could Peter, Major Winslow, actually *be* her beloved?

Wouldn't she recognize her beloved? Wouldn't she be attracted and fall in love instantly?

As she read the sonnet again, she sighed, her shoulders relaxing. Julia gazed out the window at clouds that shone bright white against the cerulean sky. Even the drab surroundings of the dormitory seemed a vibrant gray, blue and white. Her heart surged. Each time she finished reading the sonnet, she paused, then read again, soaking in the intense words.

***

Ann raced into the room, out of breath.

"Jules."

"What? What's wrong?"

"I'm being transferred."

"What?"

"They're transferring me to the American base hospitals in Le Tréport."

"Le Tréport? You're leaving?"

"I hadn't expected to be transferred. According to Sister Betty, the American hospital there is using all kinds of modern methods of healing, and they need assistants for training."

Julia's shoulders slumped. She didn't want Ann to leave. However, there was so much excitement in her friend's voice that Julia said, "That's swell, Ann. I shall miss you, though." Julia had heard that city's name before. "Isn't Ella the nurse we met on the ship over here, at that hospital?"

Ann sat beside Julia on the cot. "You're right. I will look her up when I arrive. But I will miss you too, Jules. Who will throw a pillow over my head when I don't wake up to the alarm?"

"I'm sure you'll find someone. When do you leave?"

"Tomorrow."

Julia pursed her lips and hugged her friend, her heart already aching. "I think you may be right, Ann."

"Right? About what?"

"About Major Winslow being my beloved. I'm not saying for certain, just open to the idea that he may be."

"Of course he is! I knew it!! He's a good man, Jules. I'll keep praying for him."

Hugging her friend tightly, Julia wished that Ann didn't have to leave.

Chapter 15
Underground

August 1, 1918

Peter turned up the oil lamp and stared at the broken fragments of his pocket watch. It had been four days since he had lost the watch. Then he found it on the grass of the barn near one of the tires of the motorcar. He must've dropped it in the barn before he had parked the car inside. He missed it for personal reasons: his father had given him the watch as a graduation gift. He also missed it for a more practical reason: time was of the utmost importance during war. Frustrated, Peter had asked Smythe to search for another timepiece. The corporal had discovered a small carriage clock on a mantle in an upstairs bedroom, still working amidst the clutter of the second floor.

He eyed the letter that Corporal Smythe had just brought to him. He was almost afraid to open it. He didn't know if he could face the rejection. Miss Julia Murphy had indeed made life worth living, even if she had no intention of any future with him other than friendship. If, as he suspected, she had no beau, he would plainly ask her if she might like to have him as her beau. Of course, it would have to wait until after the war and proper etiquette would be for him to ask her parents' permission. That might be unnecessary, however, because she had to be at least 21 to be a war volunteer.

A newly-delivered memo indicated that the Huns were on the move and at any given time, the enemy could attack.

This made it all-the more important that he refrain from moving too much about the property in case the enemy had any suspicions that the house was, in fact, an Allied post. No more use of the motorcar either since it was too noisy. Next time he needed to send Smythe out, the corporal would have to use a bicycle. The nearby village of Breilly was close enough.

Whatever content was in this letter — acceptance or rejection — he couldn't defer any longer. He tore open the letter and scanned it. Finding the words "*I do not have a beau nor do I have a beloved,*" he sighed with relief.

Peter hummed as he gazed out the window at the evening sky, reflecting on the quiet beauty of the night. Few stars twinkled but the moon shone in happiness, like an intense, bright light.

This would be his opportunity.

Dear Miss Murphy,

I am pleased to receive your latest letter and especially happy to hear that, as pretty and kind as you are, no man has yet captured your heart.

Say, you haven't given a pocket watch away recently, have you? It seems like every time I'm in need of an item, I receive it indirectly from you. That would certainly be swell, seeing as how mine recently broke. Of course, I digress.

I end, once again, with a sonnet written only for you:

Julia's Gifts

No Light of Stars, Nor Moon

In night as deep as eye can throw its gaze,
This cavern sky whose wall one cannot grope
Does offer fair display of ease and hope;
A dusted light to which our spirits raise.

Now, ruddy does the leading role present,
Soon gold, and then bright white, arrives on high.
Then half the canopy expires a sigh,
And at the pleading of the orb are sent.

And so, alone, the moon and I reflect
Upon the light that he and I respect;
The hope that burning love will have its day.
No light of stars, nor moon, nor all collect,
Be light enough or pure enough bedeck'd,
As the glow of my beloved's fair array.

*I would be honoured if you said yes to the following
question: would you allow me to be your beloved?*

Peter

***

The next morning, Corporal Smythe packed small
boxes and correspondence in a basket attached to the
bicycle. The letters and items needed to be sent by post to
Allied Headquarters in Paris. Then he patted the major's
personal letter in his breast pocket and smiled. The major's
morale had lifted considerably since he commenced
writing to Miss Murphy of the field hospital near Soissons.
Of course, after seeing the girl a few weeks ago, Major
Winslow was no longer sullen. In fact, the major smiled

more, and from time to time, the corporal could hear him humming.

He pedaled along the dirt roads, keeping watch to his surroundings.

As he got closer to the village, there was an explosion ahead of him on the road. The corporal jammed on his brakes to avoid the hole in the road. There was nowhere to steer, however, to avoid the regimen of Huns attacking him from the front. He and the bike plunged into the ditch, his leg twisted and caught under the bike. Smythe tried to raise his hands in surrender, but it was too late. His body was riddled with bullets and, in the last few seconds of his life, the bicycle was ripped from his body.

***

Where is Smythe? He should've returned hours ago. This afternoon's message from headquarters warned him that German troops were in the vicinity, so he should proceed to the bunker. Worried for the corporal, he found himself praying for the man. Peter's anger at God had turned into hope and trust that the war would end soon — and that perhaps he and Julia might find a way to be together.

He gathered all papers, equipment, more food, water, oil for the lamp and an extra flashlight, and any other evidence that Allies had been at the farmhouse. Then he patted Coquette. He hated to leave the dog behind, but animals could be very resourceful. He hoped now that she was stronger, she might survive any surrounding artillery fire. He had already placed extra food beside her because he would not be able to feed her over the next few days, maybe weeks.

Peter then headed to the basement. He clicked the lever

behind the bookcase and the door opened. He stepped into the room, then closed the door carefully so as to not disturb the books.

He lit the oil lamp and shone it on the shelves. He took inventory of supplies: biscuits, tea, water, tinned meat and Maconochie stew — which he detested, but it was food, and he would rather eat it than starve. And he certainly didn't look forward to using a hole in the floor to relieve himself.

Peter carried the lamp to the table. Before he could set it down, the ground trembled. Then the growing hum of engines broke the silence. Enemy trucks.

Peter's heart skipped a beat and he looked up, though the bunker had no windows.

Perhaps Smythe couldn't make it back into the area. And if he did make it to the post office, would he know *not* to return?

I've only got provisions for two weeks, so I'll need to ration them. And only one bottle of oil for the lamp, as well as ten candles and a flashlight.

Of course, the basement room had been built to keep the equipment and intelligence messages safe. Peter was a realist and knew that to the Allied forces, it was of little importance that he remained unharmed. That was part of war.

He set up the machine to listen to incoming messages. Then he contacted the Allies through the communications system. The "hello girls" as they were called, were bubbly Americans who would connect him to someone in charge. He would also have to give the correct password.

"Hello?"

"Yes. My name is Major Peter Winslow, Canadian Expeditionary Forces, serial number 27458."

There was silence on the other end of the phone.

"Miss? Hello?"

It sounded like she was clearing her throat. "Uh, yes, I'm so sorry. Go on."

"Please tell Commander Foch that I am safe and continuing to translate."

"Yes, Major." The girl paused. "Are...are you related to Staff Sergeant John Winslow?"

Peter drew in a breath. "Yes, yes, I am. Did you know my brother?"

"Yes, I..." She paused. "I was with your brother when he passed away."

Peter couldn't speak for a moment but willed himself to ask her the question. "Are you...Laura? How...did he die? The letter said the church was bombed."

"Yes, I'm Laura. And, yes, that's right. We both made it out alive, but John kept returning to save four children and their mother. He wouldn't stop until every one of them was safe. He had just handed the mother to another soldier and turned to go back in to see if anyone else needed assistance when," her voice trembled, "the entire roof fell on him. They assured me that he died instantly."

Peter couldn't form words, so he remained silent. His brother had survived the initial bombing, only to go back in and save multiple people before dying.

"Major?"

"Yes, yes, I'm here. Thank you. Thank you for letting

me know. We can't stay on too long. Just let Commander Foch know that I am alive and will remain here until it's safe to emerge. Please also tell him that my assistant, Corporal Andrew Smythe, set out on bicycle at 0800 hours via back roads to take correspondence and packages to the post office in Breilly. He has yet to return."

"Yes, Major."

Peter was still trying to comprehend the last moments of his brother's life. God *had* protected John, but his selfless and generous brother had given his life to save others.

Chapter 16
Prayers for
Major Winslow

With the sheer numbers of wounded coming in on a daily basis, Julia was assigned to the dreaded death ward along with her friend Charlotte. Julia could not fathom how the girl seemed to get through each day holding dying men's hands. And Charlotte seemed to find her purpose in life here among the dying. Earlier this morning, Charlotte was singing quietly to one of the soldiers as he gasped one last time.

Julia admired Charlotte, but she had gone from animated and engaging to intense and somber since Dr. K had been transferred. But then again, the war changed people in unexpected ways. Although Charlotte had said nothing to her, Julia suspected that she had grown fond of Dr. K, especially after spending five harrowing days with the doctor during the July siege at the field hospital.

But Julia was lonely for her dearest friend, Ann, and perhaps somewhat envious. From Ann's letters, Le Tréport sounded like a beautiful spot at the top of a cliff that looked out onto the ocean. Julia had to admit that, right about now, she would appreciate a change of scenery.

In the past few days that she had been working in this ward, Julia had grown quite fond of Eddie, an 18-year-old from Idaho. The young soldier had suffered from lung damage due to gas inhalation, as well as septicemia from having an open wound in the muddy trench before he could be transported to a field hospital. Eddie always smiled when she came to check on him. Today, he was quiet, eyes half-open, staring, glistening with tears.

"Good afternoon, Eddie. Is there anything I can do for you today?"

"Yes, ma'am." He forced a smile. "When I'm gone, would you write to my mother and tell her I didn't suffer and that I love her," he paused. "And that the hardest part is that I'll never be able to say those words again?"

Julia bit her lip to fight back the tears. "Let's write your mother a letter now, so that the words she reads are yours."

He nodded and Julia wrote down his words in a letter to his mother. She placed it in an envelope, addressed it and had it ready for when Pierre came to collect the mail.

When Julia returned to the soldier's bedside, she found that Eddie's skin was ashen, a sign that his time was near. Charlotte sat beside him and tenderly held onto his hand.

"Charlotte?"

"Hmm?" The girl was gazing intently into the young soldier's eyes.

"I would like to hold Eddie's hand, if you don't mind."

She looked up, her eyes widening. "Of course, Julia." Charlotte released the boy's hand, stood and allowed Julia to sit on the edge of the cot. Charlotte remained behind Julia for a few moments before someone called her name and she left.

Over the next hour, Julia clung onto the boy's hand. His hand gradually lost its tight grasp. Eddie's breathing became irregular; he gasped for one final breath, then he was gone.

Julia's eyes glistened. Standing up, she said a silent prayer for his soul and gently covered his head with a sheet.

Death and destruction, torn-off limbs, gaping wounds, lungs, kidneys, burned skin. Julia no longer wanted to see the wretched consequences of war. She was tired of breathing in the pungent odor of burning flesh and blood.

She stepped outside the barrack, held her hands to her face and wept. Someone touched her shoulder. She turned to see that Charlotte had followed her outside. The two girls embraced, their sorrows bursting forth in an ocean of tears.

***

Over the ensuing six days, Peter remained grateful that he still had a way to communicate with the outside world from the hidden room in the basement. He continued to hope and pray that Smythe had made it to town before the enemy had arrived. If Smythe hadn't made it...Peter couldn't think of the alternative.

In all that time, he never heard Coquette bark or whine. He hoped that she was safe.

Peter had also had nearly a week to reflect on his life and faith. Why had Peter assumed that God hadn't answered his prayers? He *had* answered his prayer and protected John. It was *John* who had chosen to be a hero.

From time to time, Peter could hear Huns walking above him on the road. Given his close proximity to the front, he was able to intercept the constant messages relayed between enemy battalions. The Huns were still on the defensive, and Peter knew there was a secret Allied offensive planned to catch them off guard. If all went as planned, it would happen at 0400 hours the following day. He looked at the clock in the dim light of the room. It was now 2200 hours.

Peter hadn't realized before now that he probably had a mild case of claustrophobia. He hoped — yes, he even prayed — that the offensive would be a success, and he would be out of this awful room in the basement within the next few days.

After eating a few mouthfuls of the last tin of cold stew, he settled onto the narrow cot and tried to sleep. Drifting off, he soon began dreaming about Julia. He could almost touch her.

Ear-deafening claps and thunderous noises woke him. He had known the offensive was close, but not that close. He dragged himself from his cot, shuffled to his desk and sat down. Before he could light the oil lamp, the farmhouse exploded.

***

Julia read and re-read the two sonnets from Peter, to the point where she had memorized them. Who would've thought that the major could write so eloquently? She found herself yearning for another sonnet from him, written just for her. As each day passed, she became more and more excited at the prospect that Peter might be her beloved. Either way, each day, she offered fervent prayers for the man's safety from harm.

Chapter 17
Trapped

Peter woke to the taste of dirt in his mouth. Coughing and spewing, he couldn't believe he was still alive. The farmhouse must have taken a direct hit from above. His left leg was trapped partly under his desk — which had collapsed — and a long wooden beam that had originally been part of the ceiling. He reached his hands all around him and could feel that he was sitting on the dirt in a small open pocket. He had no light and no food.

Fast shallow breathing made him lightheaded so he forced himself to slow his breathing and relax, although trying to remain calm in this situation was nearly impossible. All he could think of were his parents who had already lost a son to this miserable war. Then he thought about Julia. At least she had made this awful war tolerable for the last few months.

Incredibly, he was able to doze off. He woke to the cool drops of rain on his face. His heart raced. How much time had passed? Blurry images surrounded him. Light came in from somewhere. Blinking rainwater from his eyes, he studied his surroundings. Beams and debris crisscrossed overhead. A ray of light streamed in through a narrow hole about eight feet above him.

The desk and a long beam pinned down his left leg. He moved his leg and winced. Peter couldn't see his leg very well, but he could feel the stinging of an open wound and hoped it wasn't broken. He moved the desk an inch at a time, until he was able to flip it off his leg.

Filled with hope, he tried to move the long beam, but it would not budge. Moist bits of dirt and misty rain splashed down onto his face and shoulder. With the one heavy beam on his leg, he still couldn't move it or much of the left half of his lower body. Peter dug his left boot heel into the dirt, praying that he could make a hole big enough to slip his leg out from under the beam. However, ten minutes of trying only made his leg burn with pain, so he ceased.

The open tin with a bit of stew lay on its side a foot or so to the right of his body. Peter reached down and grabbed it. He wasn't hungry yet — and probably would never be hungry for this dreadful stew — but he would save it for when he *was* hungry enough to eat it and use the can to get rain water for drinking.

Peter didn't know how much time had passed, but rain now poured in from the opening above and the dirt floor soon sloshed as it turned to mud. Peter again tried to dig his left boot heel into the mud. Every time he pushed his heel into the mud, his thigh burned with pain, but within a few moments, he was able to gouge out a large enough hole in the now-muddy floor.

Knowing what he had to do, he took a handkerchief from his pocket and stuffed it in his mouth. Biting down on the cloth to help control his pain, he twisted and pulled until he slipped his leg out from under the beam. Falling back, Peter released a long breath and hoped the rubble behind him didn't give way.

With his leg free, the rain seemed to slow to a drizzle. He appreciated that the muddy floor had allowed him to free his leg, but now he had to contend with trench-like conditions with both his feet ankle-deep in mud. A hot burning sensation made him steal a glimpse at his leg.

"Oh, God," he prayed aloud, overwhelmed with pain and dizzy from the sight. Muscle and bone showed through his torn pant leg and jagged skin. Blood oozed from the long wound. He took his belt off and clamped it around his upper thigh to slow the bleeding.

Numbing himself from the pain, Peter used the near-empty tin to collect water and drank as much as his stomach would allow him.

There wasn't much he could do now. He had to try to distract himself. He lifted out the journal and pencil from his front coat pocket. He wrote on the first page of the booklet: *If found, please send to Miss Julia Murphy, Soissons Field Hospital, France.*

***

News of the Allied offensive made Julia hopeful that the war would end soon. The middle of August brought cooler nights and mornings, although the afternoons were still quite warm.

For the past day or so, Julia had been given a particularly heart-wrenching task: preparing deceased soldiers for burial. It entailed removing all items from the pockets and ensuring each man was identified so that the families back home could be apprised of the soldier's resting place. Most Allied soldiers who died in France also remained here for burial.

With the decrease in numbers of live casualties and the increase in dead soldiers, their field hospital now had an entire area outside set up between two barracks for preparing the dead for burial. Julia didn't like it, but she treated each body with respect and reverence, reciting a prayer over each man.

A *camion* arrived later that day with a group of deceased Allied soldiers.

"Miss?"

Julia turned to see two Canadian soldiers with a body on a stretcher. The smell emanating from the body made Julia's eyes water and she blinked, then squinted.

"Sorry for the stench, Miss, but this is one of our own. We brought him to the stationary hospital near Amiens, close to where he was found, but they were trying to handle only live casualties and told us they wouldn't be able to bury him for a while, so we brought him here. He has been missing for a few weeks." The man put his hand to his nose. "Unfortunately, it looks as though he has been dead the entire time. This isn't going to be a pleasant task. However, Corporal Smythe was an exemplary soldier. We'd like to bury him as soon as possible and let his family know that he's no longer missing in action."

"Yes, of course." She stopped. "Did you say the man's name was Smythe?"

"Yes."

"Corporal Smythe is Major Winslow's assistant."

"I believe that's right."

Julia's ears began to ring and she couldn't move. Her mouth was open, but no words would form. She had met this man a little over a month ago. *Dear God, if he is dead, where is Peter?* She stood still, hands shaking, until one of the Canadian soldiers spoke.

"Miss?"

She blinked and pointed. "Uh...yes. Over there," she motioned for them to place the corporal's body on the wooden table. "Thank you, sirs. I will take good care of him."

Her hands still trembling, Julia wrapped a linen mask over her mouth and pinned it at the back of her head. *Where is Peter?* Her usually strong stomach churned and the handkerchief over her face did little to keep the strong odor of decomposition from her nostrils. She put on another pair of gloves, doubled the linen cloth over her nose and mouth and set to work. The young soldier's body had been riddled with bullets, and insects filled many wounds.

First, Julia reached into the pockets of his pants — or what was left of them — and pulled out various coins, keys and other small items. Then she noticed there was something sticking out of the front pocket of his jacket. She carefully removed what appeared to be an envelope — a letter — from the man's pocket. She held it in her hands. It was stained in this poor soldier's blood. Could this be to his sweetheart? She stared, trying to decipher what was written on the envelope.

The first word was "Miss" but the next word was a bit more difficult to read through the stains. J...u...l...i...a M...u...r — she gasped, her mouth open, and she nearly dropped the envelope. *Oh, dear God!*

Heart racing and hands shaking, Julia again looked down and the writing seemed clear as day. *"Miss Julia Murphy, c/o Soissons Field Hospital."* Scanning to the left, amidst the reddish-brown stains, she could just make out the name *Winslow* in the upper left-hand corner.

"Did you find something important?" one of the Canadian soldiers asked.

Julia nodded but could barely speak. "I...um...may

I...may I have this? I am...Julia Murphy. I know Major Winslow. This is *my* letter."

"Aye, Miss. Just let me take a look at it first to make sure there isn't any military information." She gave him the envelope. He took out the letter and squinted as he read. "Here, Miss. It's hard to read, but..." The man handed it to her. "It's fine."

"Thank you." Julia gathered the rest of the items from Smythe's pockets, put them in a marked bag, and covered the corporal's body in a linen sheet. "Corporal Smythe is ready for burial. You may take him to the cemetery nearby. I believe they are burying yesterday's dead."

After the men left with Smythe's body, Julia covered her eyes with her hands and wept. This young corporal had been killed in action with Peter's letter to her in his pocket. The corporal's blood was on the letter so she opened it reverently, hoping she would still be able to read the words.

***

Peter had already filled up the journal with poems and writings to Julia. It not only helped to pass the time, but it distracted him from his pain, and it gave him an opportunity to share his experiences and dreams. He wasn't surprised at how sloppy his writing was, given the lack of light and his pain. He nodded off from time to time, but the pain in his leg jarred him awake.

Julia knew what war was and if he could admit it to himself, it felt liberating to be able to tell someone else what he had been enduring. As he wrote about his time in the trenches, his eyes grew moist. The image of not one, not two, but three of his fellow comrades who were blown to pieces only a few short feet away burst into his mind.

He wrote of positive things too: his mother's delicious pot roast, mashed potatoes, baby carrots and apple crumble pie. He shared how he hoped one day she would travel with him to Arnprior. He told her that he would take her to the park and to the picture show and perhaps they could take the train to Ottawa to see the Parliament Buildings. He soon filled the entire journal and had very little graphite left. He wrote another sonnet meant only for her, then ended it with the following:

"I love you, Julia, and I pray that we will be together, but if you are reading this now, I am most likely dead. Could you please write to my family and tell them how much I love them and to be strong?"

Below that, he added his family's address in Arnprior, stuck the book back into his pocket and closed his eyes.

***

Despite the stench and stains of the letter, Julia was able to read Peter's most recent sonnet again. In the letter, he joked and asked if she had a pocket watch in her box of gifts. She couldn't believe it. A pocket watch. Another of her beloved's items that she had given away — pawned. And the sonnet, *"No Light of Stars; No Moon"* made her heart soar.

In night as deep as eye can throw its gaze,
This cavern sky whose wall one cannot grope
Does offer fair display of ease and hope;
A dusted light to which our spirits raise.

Now, ruddy does the leading role present,
Soon gold, and then bright white, arrives on high.
Then half the canopy expires a sigh,

And at the pleading of the orb are sent.

And so, alone, the moon and I reflect
Upon the light that he and I respect;
The hope that burning love will have its day.
No light of stars, nor moon, nor all collect,
Be light enough or pure enough bedeck'd,
As the glow of my beloved's fair array.

I would be honoured if you said yes to the following
question: would you allow me to be your beloved?

Peter

Peter had called her his "beloved" in this sonnet. Of course, Peter was her beloved! *Lord, thank you. Thank you for Peter. Forgive me for not realizing that he was right in front of me the whole time.* Julia had been so specific as to who her beloved *should* be and what he *should* look like that she nearly didn't recognize him.

She reached inside her box with the only remaining gift she had for her beloved, the Miraculous Medal, and put it with her Miraculous Medal on her chain. When she found Peter, this would be her gift to him. *Wherever Peter is, watch over him, Blessed Virgin. Keep this man safe. Please, please, keep him safe.*

Chapter 18
The Light of Day

As morning broke around the fifth day, Peter woke to voices above him. A wave of tension gripped him at the sound of Germans speaking to one another. He listened. They appeared to be trying to decide whether to begin searching for food amongst the ruins of the farmhouse. Finally, they moved on.

Peter hissed out a sigh. His stomach ached. At least he had been able to drink rain water on and off for the past two days. The agony in his leg made it difficult to catch his breath. He waited until last evening to eat the last mouthful from the tin of stew. And as awful as it tasted, it did silence his stomach. If anything, he hoped the end might come soon. Dying from dehydration would not be pleasant.

God, I know I don't pray very much and I don't even know if you'll hear me, but please help me get out of here. He felt strangely at peace with the entire situation, but with it, he experienced an overwhelming desire to live and to write more sonnets and to marry Julia and have a houseful of children. Children. How his parents would coddle and spoil their grandchildren. And Maggie and Dot would be doting aunts. *Please God, I want to live.*

The rumbling of planes above made him lift his chin. Was the hole above getting larger? Either he could see better because the hole was letting in more light, or he was becoming accustomed to the dark. Of course, if the hole *was* getting larger, there was a possibility that he would fall further into the ground.

Within this pocket of air, he tried lifting himself ever so slowly to get to that hole above him. With each movement, he prayed for freedom. All he needed was to get out of the hole. Breathing became more difficult now, but Peter did his best not to take deep breaths. He climbed a few feet, but fatigue prevented him from going higher. Balancing himself on wood and stone, he leaned forward to take a break.

***

While Julia was cleaning a soldier's wounds, her mind drifted to Peter. Now that Julia was convinced that Peter was her beloved, was he even alive? The young corporal was dead. Had Peter died with him? If so, why hadn't they brought his body in with the corporal's? Peter's letters and moving sonnets were so beautiful and intense with emotion. She could feel his presence with each word. *No, he isn't dead.*

That day, whenever Julia tenderly cleaned a soldier or gave one a hypodermic or prepared a man for the operating theater, each became Peter. Julia needed faith that her beloved was alive and being treated with compassion and kindness.

***

Peter couldn't believe it. His hand actually reached the opening of the hole in the dirt above him. As much as he wanted to climb out, he couldn't rush his movements. First, he didn't have the stamina. Second, doing so could bring all the dirt and debris back down upon him. It was dusk and he wanted to make it out during the cover of darkness.

The ground shuddered as a vehicle drove over the road nearby, and Peter slipped back down a foot or so, moving beyond the reach of the hole. He gritted his teeth, hissing out a swear word.

The battle was close enough that Peter could hear the shots and cannons, but he could now barely lift his head. He would give anything to have a canteen of water — or better yet, an ice cold mug of Molson's beer.

Peter hadn't eaten very much and most of the time, when the agonizing pain in his leg allowed him to nod off, he dreamt of home. Maybe he would have to surrender to the weakness — and to death — if it came. But he wasn't ready to give up. There were so many things he still wanted to accomplish with his life.

As dawn broke, the hole above him appeared wider and the sun shone on his face. *Only two feet above me.* Of course, it might've been forty feet for all Peter could manage. He owed it to his parents and sisters — and Julia — to make his best effort to get out. He stepped on a pile of rubble near the opening, moved some of the rocks, bricks and pieces of wood until he was nearly able to stand and stick his head out of the hole.

But as he stood up, the ground below him gave way. His stomach leaped and arms shot out. Panicked, he groped through shifting dirt and debris until finally latching onto something secure.

If I can just lift myself up and out of the hole...

***

Every time Julia heard about another battle being won by the Allies, she felt sure that the war was nearing its end. If the war ended, how would she find Peter? And why had she not received any other letters — or sonnets — from him? Again, she touched the medals on her chain and recited a silent *Hail Mary* for his safety.

***

Exhausted, Peter could no longer hold his body up. He was nauseated and dizzy and could barely see straight, let alone hold his body in place. Despite the fire of pain in his leg, he had the chills. It was summer, but he was freezing. *What's the use? I can't do this any longer. I'm not going to be able to get out. I might as well let go.*

Then he heard Maggie's voice inside his head. *Don't you dare die, Pete. No matter what! Come back to us alive!*

In that moment, Peter forced his eyes open. He must try, even if he failed. He forced his weary arms overhead and grabbed onto a beam with one hand and a hunk of brick with the other. "For you, Maggie," he mumbled. He shoved his foot into more debris and pulled himself up six inches. "For you, Mum, Dad and Dot." Another half-foot. Every inch of his body ached and he wanted to rebel. But he *could* do this. He *would* do this.

"And, Julia, for you," he said, breathless. Using every ounce of strength, Peter gained another few inches. He steadied himself, then — with what seemed to be more strength than he had in days — he pulled himself up and out of the hole.

He collapsed onto the pile of rubble, hoping it wouldn't give way. He tried to stay still. The sun's rays on his face and body soothed and warmed him and he no longer felt cold. Weak and barely able to move, the laceration on his leg exploding with pain, Peter dozed off.

***

Peter woke to laughter but was too weak to open his

eyes. Then, realizing he was hearing German, he hoped the Huns would think he was dead. He tried to remain as still as possible.

He could hear them speaking in German talking about killing 'Amis.' *Each of them wants to kill one more American.*

"Ah, what do we have here?"

"Canadian. Not worth it. He's dead anyway."

"Canadian, American, close enough."

Peter heard a gun cock and, remaining as still as possible, prepared for the end.

***

Julia had just come from the barracks and was walking toward the *château* when she heard a loud pop behind her. Taking a deep breath and closing her eyes, she slowly turned to see what it was. Before her eyes could focus on the figure on the ground, someone screamed. *Please, let it not be another...* She stared down at a soldier who had just committed suicide — likely a victim of shell shock — his body a crumpled mass of legs and arms.

Please take care of Peter, God. Please watch over my beloved and keep him safe.

Chapter 19
Alive

A dog whined. Something warm and wet brushed across Peter's cheek. Barking made his eyes blink and he squinted at a blue sky. He was too weak to do anything, but Coquette was licking his face. *Glad to see you too, girl.* Above him was blue sky. Was this heaven? Surely he must be dead. The Hun soldier had just shot him. *Wait...a dog...in heaven?*

He took a deep breath and gasped in pain. It felt like someone had stabbed the left side of his chest. And his leg continued to burn with pain. In heaven, he wouldn't feel pain, would he? No, he was not dead. He was definitely experiencing pain.

Peter stuck his hand down his shirt to feel the skin of his chest. It was sticky. Pulling his hand out, there was blood on his fingers.

He was bleeding, but he was alive. *God, I'm not sure how you're going to do it, but I need to get to a hospital quickly.* He no longer heard or felt Coquette's presence. *Where did she go?* In his weakened state, Peter's time was running out.

***

Peter drifted off again and found himself back home in Arnprior with his family. John and Peter were teasing Maggie who was saying, "You're all right, Major." *Why was Maggie saying such strange things?*

Then Peter felt himself being lifted up and onto something. A woman's voice. "He's ready to be transported to the field hospital."

Another man's voice. "No, not to a field hospital. This officer's leg needs immediate medical attention. He's also got a chest wound. We're taking all officers to the Canadian Base Hospital in Le Tréport."

Peter opened his eyes. He was in some sort of a vehicle, a closed truck. "Thirsty," was all he could moan.

"Not yet, Major," a man replied. "We'll reach the hospital in Le Tréport shortly. We'll get you fixed up there."

In his cloud of unconsciousness, it sounded like the man laughed. "Major, you have a mongrel dog to thank. She alerted us that you were here."

Coquette. Bless her.

"My book, my...j...journal."

"Where is it, Major?"

"Breast...poc...ket."

The man gasped. "Holy moly. You took a direct hit there, sir!" Peter felt the man opening his shirt. "And looks like it went clear through the book and into your chest. The bullet's still there but the wound doesn't appear to be deep. This journal probably saved your life, Major. That and the dog. You must have someone looking out for you." Peter nodded, then felt the man lift the book from his pocket. *Where did he put it? If he didn't survive, he wanted...Julia to have it. She must...*

"Please, give it to...I need you to give it to Jul..." Peter slipped into unconsciousness.

***

In Le Tréport, Ann had just finished a shift at the

venereal diseases ward and was heading back to the American dormitory tents on the other side of the complex. One of the aspects of her current posting that she didn't like very much was that the American dorm was half-a-mile away. Her feet always hurt at the end of a shift, but she tried to stop at various places along the way. This hospital complex happened to be situated at the top of a cliff overlooking the water. Le Tréport Base was, in fact, a small city which included four stationary hospitals, three YMCA buildings, a cinema, a canteen, a post office and two churches as well as a recreation area. Ann had never seen anything like it and was especially excited last week when she used the *funiculaire* railway to go through a tunnel in the cliff and down to the beach.

Ann enjoyed being able to spend time with Ella again. She and Ella had spent the afternoon together during a quiet day in fighting. Ella had shared with her that she had met a kind and handsome soldier. Yesterday, Ella left suddenly without saying goodbye.

She passed the post office on her way back to the dorm. Ann decided to stop to see if there were any letters waiting for her. The young French man on duty already knew Ann's name. "Bonjour, Mam'selle. You have 'nother letter."

"Wonderful. Thank you!"

He handed her the letter, and she saw that it was from Julia.

After, "I miss you," Julia had inserted many exclamation points. Well, Ann missed her friend, too. She enjoyed her new posting at the American Hospital in Le Tréport because of the location near the ocean. She didn't enjoy her job here, though. She had been assigned to the

VD ward. She would have preferred to stay where she was and help men with wounds caused by serving bravely rather than contracted through illicit behavior.

As she passed No. 2 Canadian General Hospital, she noticed a small brown book lying on the grass. Something looked odd about it. Scanning the area, Ann saw no one around to claim the book. She crouched down and picked it up. Realizing what she looked at, she gasped. A hole went straight through it. Was that — she dropped the book.

Blood — still wet — clung to its cover. The owner of this book must be dead. If not dead, then mortally wounded.

She couldn't stop staring at it, though. Had she seen this journal before? It had a leaf on the — *Oh, Lord.* Picking it up again, she opened it. She could just make out, *"Dearest Julia"* and drew in a breath. Could this be? On the inside front cover, she read, *"Julia, if you are reading this, I am likely dead, so please..."* Some of the words were made illegible by the stains or missing because of the bullet hole. *"If found, please give this book to Miss Julia Murphy, care of Soissons Field Hospital."*

"Dear Lord in heaven. This *is* Major Winslow's journal and...one of Julia's gifts for her beloved." Ann pursed her lips and blinked the tears away. She knew what she had to do, as difficult as it would be. She would keep the journal and give it to Julia *after* the war. There was no sense in her knowing the major's fate right now, not this close to the end of the war. She held it to her chest as if it were a priceless jewel, not caring about the blood that still smeared its cover.

***

It was already August 21st and Julia had received no letters, no poems, no correspondence at all from Major Winslow since the letter that was found on Corporal Smythe, dated August 1st. All Julia had were four short letters (one stained with blood) and three exquisite sonnets.

Descending the staircase, Julia headed to the death ward to speak with Charlotte. Sister Betty called to her. "Miss Murphy, the American hospital in Le Tréport needs more girls. I'll be sending you and a few of the other medical aid volunteers there to help. The enemy is pulling back, but there are increased casualties in that area."

"Yes, ma'am." Julia was happy to be going to the city where Ann and Ella were, but what if Major Winslow sent her a letter here? Would they forward her mail to the new hospital? Of course, they would.

Excitement was building within her as she closed her suitcase. In less than an hour, she had already packed everything from her cot. She raced outside to the death ward to say goodbye to Charlotte.

"You're leaving?"

Julia nodded. "Going to Le Tréport, where Ann and Ella are."

Charlotte lowered her head. Then she lifted her chin. "I wish you didn't have to go."

"I know."

"I shall be brave, dear Julia. And I will pray for Major Winslow."

"Thank you." Julia embraced her friend. "And I will pray for you." Charlotte was hugging her so tightly that

Julia could barely breathe. Finally, Julia pulled away. "Godspeed, Charlotte."

Back outside, she and the two other girls waited near the entrance to the *château*. The *camion* finally arrived and the girls got in and headed for the train station in Soissons.

They would travel by train first to Amiens, and then to Le Tréport.

On the train, Julia turned and gazed out the window. As they passed through Compiegne, bombed-out churches and other buildings seemed to be the normal scene amidst the people walking and talking and carrying on as usual.

Out of the city, though, Julia nodded off, then woke abruptly as the train slowed down. She looked out the window and drew in a breath. An entire field of poppies, red as blood, stretched on until the horizon. So much beauty amidst so much destruction. So much life amidst so much death. Julia softened as she thought of herself and Charlotte. Even through all the devastation around them, nature continued moving forward. *Please, God, let the war end soon. And please keep Peter safe.*

***

Peter woke up on his back. His leg was still exploding with pain. His chest felt like someone had inserted a hand and rearranged his insides. He tried opening his eyes, but even that seemed strenuous. Despite his weakness, he began to shiver. And he was so thirsty. If he only had a sip of water.

"Wa...ter," he whispered.

Someone put a hand on Peter's forehead. "Oh, my dear, you're burning up." The girl had a British accent.

He opened his eyes a sliver, the bright room making him squint. "Julia. Jule..."

"Is that your sweetheart? My name is Sister Wendy. This is the No. 2 Canadian General Hospital at Le Tréport."

"My...my journal...where is..."

"Your journal? Would it be in the clothing you came in with?"

Peter shook his head and whispered, "Some...one...took it. Julia...I want..." Weak and dizzy, all he could do was close his eyes and surrender to the weakness.

Peter was in a beautiful field with long grass blowing in the wind, corn fields on either side of him. A girl strolled toward him but she was too far away to identify. As she got closer, she was just as he remembered her: the sweet smile, beautiful dark hair and intense brown eyes.

Peter roused as someone was moving him. In a fog of semi-consciousness, he heard a jumble of words: "surgery, leg infected, amputation."

He heard the words but couldn't comprehend what they meant. "I...I want to live."

"Yes, Major. We're going to do our best to save your life."

***

The *camion* had picked up the girls at the train station and had driven so quickly and so erratically all over the road (avoiding holes) that Julia wondered whether they would arrive in one piece. It finally rode through the gates of Le Tréport base hospital, which was a huge compound of several hospitals and hundreds of barracks. She craned her neck and could see the beautiful Hotel Trianon which, she was told, was now a British-run hospital.

They finally rolled through the gates. Julia had no sooner stepped down from the vehicle when a tall, older woman grabbed her arm. "You've arrived! This way," she said, with her Boston accent. Julia glanced back at her two comrades as the three of them were racing — and stumbling — to keep up with this woman. Her original plan of reuniting with Ann and Ella would have to wait.

"You girls have been sent to us because you have already had influenza. We need your help in the influenza tents." Julia breathed a sigh of relief. There were worse assignments, like cleaning out pus-filled wounds, trying to remove mud caked on like plaster and peeling clothes off the gas-burned body of a soldier.

***

Peter roused, but his eyes remained closed. He still felt a dull ache in his chest and his leg was burning, although it didn't seem as bad. Hopefully, they had given him morphine. His tongue, thick and dry, made it impossible to speak.

"Major, you're awake!"

His eyes opened to a slit. A heavyset older nurse was leaning over him, her face too close to his. The woman had an Irish — or perhaps Newfoundland — accent and wore a wide grin. "How are you feeling?"

He opened his mouth to speak, but he could only grunt.

"You've been unconscious for ten days. The doctors were finally able to get your infection under control and they saved your leg. You're very, very lucky."

Lucky, but broken. And alive.

"Are you hungry?"

He nodded and swallowed, but his tongue was as thick as leather.

"I'll bring you some broth. By the way, my name's Sadie. If you want to be formal, it's Sister Sadie."

He forced a smile. Broth. Why couldn't he have real food, like steak and potatoes or Shepherd's Pie? Or better yet, *tourtière*. The nurse said he was unconscious for more than a week, and he hadn't eaten much since the bunker was bombed. No wonder he was weak. But his head was clearer and when he opened his eyes wider, he took in his surroundings. He was in a hospital. The building was larger. The clean white walls, neat curtains between the cots, and modern lights indicated he wasn't at a field hospital in Soissons.

Immediately, Julia's face appeared in his mind. Was she still near Soissons?

***

Ten straight days of working in the influenza ward was beginning to take its toll on Julia. It was now the last day of August. Men were continuing to die from this awful flu — strong men — some of who had already survived gas or other serious war wounds.

More often than not, men were vomiting on the floor, on the beds, on themselves and on the volunteers — anywhere but in basins. The wretched stench hung in the air and in her nose, no matter where she was, even when she was back at her sleeping quarters.

Sleeping quarters? Since she had arrived, she had slept

no more than two or three hours each night. Besides, it took a half hour just to walk to the other side of the compound to her dorm. She hadn't yet seen Ann or Ella, let alone found time to visit with them. Julia hadn't any time to think of anything — except for Peter. She thought of him when she cared for each patient. From time to time, she touched the medals — his medal in particular — on her chain.

There were many good provisions at this hospital: the food, the accommodations, even privacy screens around the cots. One of the other volunteers told her that there was even a cinema, a post office and churches here. Since this was a stationary hospital, the meals were more substantial and the bread — albeit without butter — was fresh-baked and tasted heavenly.

By early afternoon, only nine men remained in the ward. The supervisor told Julia to go and sleep and be back by midnight. When she finally got to the dorm, she tried to sleep, but instead, tossed and turned. It didn't help that it was afternoon, and girls were coming in and out of the large barrack-dorm.

Julia got up and decided to explore the hospital compound. Since the small Catholic church was right beside the American dorms, she walked in that direction. It had been a long time since she had been in church — or at least a church that wasn't in danger of having the roof cave in. From the outside, it looked like a regular long barrack, except that it had a cross at the top of it and a sign saying "Catholic Church" on the front. She opened the door and saw a few soldiers and nurses kneeling inside in peaceful silence. Seeing the tabernacle candle lit, she knew that Christ was present. Dipping her finger in the holy water font, she blessed herself, genuflected and knelt near a chair in the back.

***

Morphine helped to alleviate Peter's pain, but he insisted emphatically that he be only given the minimum dosage. His allotment would last longer if he suffered through the pain now. The morphine was enough to take the edge off, but it still hurt like hell. The chest wound notwithstanding, it felt like someone had cut off his leg, then stitched it back on.

"Major, here is some beef broth for you to sip." Sadie was leaning over and about to set it on the small table beside his bed.

He groaned. "Sadie, honey, I need real food. Please. Something with substance."

"Not until you've voided twice. Sorry, Major."

Admittedly, even though he had consumed three bowlfuls of broth so far, he hadn't yet urinated. He wasn't looking forward to Sadie holding a basin under him so he could relieve himself.

"Want to try now?" Sadie held out a basin and Peter cringed. There was no way he was going to get around this. She swiped the curtain around the bed for privacy, but for Peter, his embarrassment was working its way from his toes to his reddened face.

Chapter 20
Lost and Found

Feeling refreshed — at least spiritually — Julia stepped out of the chapel barrack and wondered where to explore next. Since the American dorms were so close, perhaps she would ask some of the other nurses and volunteers if they knew who and where Ann was. Her plan was to find Ann before dinner, then return to the dorm to rest before going back on shift at midnight. Julia couldn't wait to see Ann's face!

She passed a few girls and asked them if they knew Ann Fremont. They didn't, at least not by name. She was about to go inside one of the dorm barracks when she heard her name. Julia turned.

Ann stood at a distance with her hands over her mouth and her eyes wide. "Jules! Oh my goodness!" She took off running and the two girls embraced. "You're here? Have you been transferred??"

"Yes. I'm working in the influenza ward! I've been here for over a week but haven't had a moment to look for you."

"No kidding!! That's swell!! I can't wait to have some visiting time. I want you to come and ride down to the beach with me on the *funiculaire*."

"The what?"

"The car that takes us from here down to the shore area."

"Yes, that sounds keen."

"Are you free for an hour or so, or must you return immediately?" Ann asked.

"I'm available until midnight, although I should return by dinner time so I can rest before my next shift."

"Allow me to go to my dormitory and change."

"Of course."

"Come on."

When Julia stepped into Ann's sleeping quarters, she opened her mouth in surprise. It was even more spacious than her barrack at the other end of the block. Like in her own quarters, each cot had its own privacy divider. Julia would never again take her privacy for granted. So many days, she had wished to close herself in a closet, just to be alone with her thoughts. And here, she and Ann now had as close to that as she could imagine.

"Aren't these dividers heavenly, Ann?"

"Yes, they are."

The girls moved forward to Ann's private area, and Julia sat on the bed, allowing her eyes to wander. Ann took off her coat and hung it on a hook near the wall.

On Ann's bedside table was a familiar brown journal with dark stains and — *my God!* Her heart beat wildly, and her head grew light. That was — *it had to be* — the journal that she had originally bought for her beloved, the one that had been given to Peter! A small hole went through the book — a bullet hole? She could still see the maple leaf embossed on the front.

Her mouth was open, but she couldn't speak. Finally, her voice shaking, she said, "I...uh...Ann, what is Peter's journal doing on your nightstand?"

Ann's face blanched, and she moved swiftly to the table and slipped the book inside the drawer. "Oh, that's nothing, just a —"

Julia pushed her friend aside, yanked open the drawer and lifted up the journal. Paging through, she found blood and writing — Peter's — on the pages inside.

She scanned through page after page, only able to read a few lines at a time, given the stains and the hole through the middle. On the front inside cover, Peter had indicated that he wanted her to have this journal. *Oh dear. Peter, what has happened to you?* She flipped through the blood-stained pages. On the last page, written in unsteady script was another sonnet. The bullet had gone through the blank space in between the stanzas. The sonnet was blood-stained, but intact. She held her breath as she read.

On Wings of Dove

Look skyward, fellow worshipers of Light,
Your gaze not fixed upon these walls so near
Of this unsightly catacomb of fear;
This dark cathedral where endure we night.

The blood-stained windows of our beaten souls
Dim all attempts of dawn's warm rays to cheer,
And broken buttress, barely standing sheer,
Press into mire and gouge their hellish holes.

> *But o, ye dome of holy light above,*
> *Couldst thou on weary soldier now bestow*
> *An apparition? Lo, her face aglow!*
> *'T'would make my heart to rise on wings of dove*
> *And dream myself into her arms of love,*
> *Lest burrow I here in despair below.*

Shaking her head, she sniffed, trying desperately not to weep. "Where...did you...get this, Ann?"

Ann lowered her head. She was silent for a moment, then whispered, "I found it on the ground outside of one of the medical barracks. Look at this bullet hole." She pointed. "And he wrote, *'Julia, if you're reading this, I am most likely dead.'* Jules, he couldn't have survived an injury like this, could he?"

Julia began to tremble, and a cold, hard knot formed in the pit of her stomach. Then she shook her head. No, she would not give in to despair. "Of course, he could survive! And...well, we don't even know if *he* was the one that was shot."

"Be realistic, Jules. This is war, not a fairy tale. And Major Winslow himself says he is most likely dead."

Julia stared at the book in her hands, her gaze latching onto one of the thick brown stains. Clearly, someone had lost blood with this injury. There was only one way to find out.

"Where?"

"Where what?"

"Take me to the place where you found it."

"But Jules..."

"Please," she begged, "take me there, even if what we discover is bad."

Desperate to know, Julia grabbed onto Ann's hand. She began to run, tugging Ann with her. "Quickly, please!" Finally, Ann began to sprint with Julia alongside her. When they reached one of the barracks of the Canadian-run hospital, Ann slowed and came to a stop. She pointed to the ground near a window beside the door. "This is where I found it."

Julia stared at the grass, its leaves pointing heavenward, no indication that anything as important as this journal had once been there.

She opened the door and could feel Ann's breath right behind her.

"Jules...."

Shaking her head, Julia rushed to the first nurse she could find. "Major Peter Winslow, is he in this barrack?"

The plump, older nurse's brows straightened. "I don't think so, dear, at least not now." Her voice was filled with empathy.

"Might he have been brought here from the front?"

"Possibly, but if he needed surgery, he would be in another barrack now, recuperating."

"Please, could you check for me?"

The woman glanced down at the man she was tending. He was unconscious, and she had been cleaning his leg wound. "I would be happy to do that for you, but allow me to finish with this gentleman first."

"Of course. Thank you so much. We'll wait outside."

Julia stared again at the blood-stained journal. If —
and it was a big if — this *was* Peter's blood, he still could
be alive. She would not lose hope, not now.

***

The middle-aged, heavyset nurse finally emerged from
the barrack and faced Julia and Ann. "I don't have
anything here for a Major Winslow, but he may have been
transferred to another barrack. But if he was at this
barrack, he is likely still in this general vicinity. Unless... "

"Unless what?"

"Well, unless he...well, you know, died."

Julia's fists clenched and she lowered her head.

Ann put her hand on Julia's back. "I'm sorry, Jules. I
didn't write to you about finding his journal because I
believed he was dead. I didn't want you to know. Not until
the end of the war."

"This *is* his journal — the one that was originally my
beloved's — but we can't know whether it's *his* blood."

"True, I suppose." Her friend sighed. "Let's try looking
for him at the convalescing barracks."

They went into four additional barracks before
someone even knew who "Major Winslow" was. A nurse
who appeared to be in her forties, Sister Wendy, nodded.
Julia just about jumped in excitement when she listened to
Sister say that Peter had been in that ward initially after he
arrived, but emergency surgery necessitated his move to
another barrack.

***

Somewhere in between urinating the first time and eating his first solid meal, weakness overcame Peter again. Later that afternoon, his head exploded in pain. It felt like someone had hammered a stake right between his eyes. He drifted in and out of consciousness and began to shiver. "Major Winslow?" He heard the girl but could not respond. Whatever was going on, surely he was dying.

Minutes — or maybe hours later — in his stupor, he heard someone say, "Influenza! Move him to the influenza wards near the convalescent camp!"

***

Julia peered at the next barrack as she and Ann strode across a strip of grass. They'd checked five barracks already. He had to be close.

Ann grabbed her arm and stopped her mid-stride. "Jules, wait."

Julia glanced at Ann then looked around, hoping Ann had seen something important. "What is it?"

"Look, it's getting late. And I need to get some sleep before my shift tomorrow. I'll ask around to see if anyone knows where the major is. And you can do the same."

"Yes, I suppose so."

"Now, Jules, my dear, let's see if we can find you a ride back to the dorm."

"No. I think I'll just walk to the influenza ward. I don't think I'll be able to sleep anyway. I might as well work."

"That's a good idea."

The girls embraced. "I'm so glad you're here, Jules.

Please forgive me for not telling you about the journal."

"Of course, Ann. I'm happy to be here, especially now that I know Peter is here."

"Jules, please..."

"I won't give up on finding him, even if..."

Ann nodded.

As they were walking away, behind them a *camion* screeched its brakes and stopped. The girls turned to see a patient being loaded into the back. Ann stopped and spoke to the driver. "Where are you taking him?"

"To the influenza ward."

"Perfect. My friend is going there. Would you mind if she rode with you?"

"Only if she's already had influenza."

"Yes, she has."

Julia spoke up. "I'm assigned to that ward."

"Hop in."

The girls said their goodbyes, exchanged a quick hug and the truck departed.

***

All of a sudden, Peter opened his mouth to retch, but there was nothing left in his stomach. He spit out a small amount of bile. Where was he? The back of a truck? He could hear chatter in front, but the pounding in his head was to the point his head would surely explode. *Dear God, have I survived just to succumb to influenza?*

***

The truck pulled to a stop and Julia thanked the British soldier. While she appreciated his familiarity and loquaciousness, she would have preferred a silent ride so she could focus on her plan to find Peter. Was he even in the city...and if he was, how critical were his wounds? She went around the back to assist the driver with unloading the critically ill soldier.

"Murphy, you're not scheduled until midnight," she heard Sister June say.

"I can't sleep. Where would you like me to go?"

"We need you in the first ward."

"Yes, all right." She turned to see Sister June accompanying the stretcher-bearers as they carried the ill soldier into the ward in front of her.

Julia followed them inside, then tripped on something on the floor. She glanced down to see what she had stepped on.

It was a muddy cap, probably from the soldier who was just transported. She picked up the hat and deposited it on a cart. Then she washed her hands at the basin nearest the door, grabbed an extra apron, and tied a mask over her face. Looking up, she could see the stretcher-bearers carrying the ill patient to the far side of the ward. *Poor man.* The ward wasn't bursting at the seams, but this barrack contained twice the numbers of ill men than it had when her shift ended hours ago. She clasped the medals on her chain. *Dear God, where is Peter? Immaculate Mary, please, please let me know where he is, even... if he is...already gone.*

***

Peter moaned as they placed him on a cot. Having no

strength to lift his head, he vomited a minute amount of bile onto the front of his shirt. He was shivering, his teeth were chattering, and his head felt like it was splitting apart. Surely, a tank was sitting on his chest.

A cold hand felt his forehead and he gasped. "He's burning up." Then he felt something stuck under his tongue. He didn't even have the strength to hold it there, and it slipped out. He nodded off in blessed oblivion.

***

Julia held the basin under the chin of an American private as he vomited. Then he pleaded for a bed pan.

"We need help over here!" Sister June yelled from across the room.

Julia scanned the ward to see if anyone would come to Sister June's aid. She couldn't move even if she wanted to, but she surmised that the poor soldier from the *camion* must be critical.

She finished assisting the American private, cleaned him up, dressed him in fresh garments and settled him on his cot.

As she straightened to leave, the soldier grabbed her skirt. "Please, please don't leave me. I'm going to die."

"Private, believe it or not, you have one of the milder cases I've seen. Your fever has already come down and your color is much better. And there's no evidence of pneumonia."

"But I feel like I'm going to die."

"I remember that feeling too. I promise to check on you as soon as I finish helping my sister nurse over there."

The man nodded and lowered his head to the pillow.

Julia removed the mask and cleaned her hands in the fresh basin nearby, making sure she scrubbed until her hands and arms felt raw. She put on a clean mask, tied it around her head, then she made her way to the critically ill patient.

***

Peter lay on a cot in a dark room. A light shone on a person approaching him. As the man came closer, Peter couldn't believe it. It was John! John was alive and vibrant and laughing beside him! Peter tried to get up off the cot, but in his weakness, he couldn't, so his brother leaned down and embraced him.

"I'm going to join you soon, John."

"No, you're not. You're going to get well and go home to Mum and Dad, Dot and Maggie. It's not your time, brother."

Peter opened his mouth to respond but his brother disappeared. Across the room, Mum, Dad, Dot and Maggie were reaching out to him, but he couldn't get up. As they backed up and faded away from him, he yelled, "Don't leave me!"

A soft voice responded, "I won't leave you, Major."

The pain in his head diminished, but his teeth chattered, and his entire body trembled. The pain in his chest made it nearly impossible to breathe, and he was suffocating. Why was it freezing cold in this ward? "C...c...cold, I'm s...s...so cold."

"Major, we're doing everything we can for you."

Chapter 21
Answered Prayers

Mask in place, Julia approached the bedside of the newly-arrived soldier. Sister June sounded somber when she whispered, "He's already progressed to pneumonia, so he won't last long. All we can do is keep him comfortable." That's when the poor soul began to have convulsions. She avoided looking at the man. It wouldn't be long now. "Julia, run next door to find a doctor. Maybe there's something he can do for this man."

Julia nodded, sad for this unfortunate soldier's family — perhaps he even had a beloved. But men died every day in this ward, and Julia could not become overemotional. Racing away from the far end of the ward, she threw open the door and ran out to the nearest barrack. Opening the door wide, she yelled, "Is there a doctor in here?"

She heard someone say, "Yes," and not waiting for him to keep up, she said, "You're needed next door."

Julia returned, out of breath, to the far corner of the ward. The man in the cot had stilled, and Sister June took his pulse. "His pulse is barely measurable."

That's when Julia looked at the man's face and screamed his name.

***

From the recesses of his mind, Peter heard Julia calling his name. But it couldn't be her voice, could it? He couldn't nod; he couldn't even open his eyes to let her know how happy — and relieved — her presence made him.

"Do — do you know this man?" Sister June asked.

"He's my — yes, I know him! He's my...beloved."

"I'm so sorry."

Julia's hand immediately went to the Miraculous Medals around her neck. It was the last of her beloved's four gifts.

Reverently, Julia lifted the chain over her head. She removed her own medal and stuffed it in her pocket, then she placed the chain with Peter's medal around his neck. The chain was short, but long enough to let the medal rest on his chest. There were no guarantees that he would recover from this virulent flu, but she wanted him to have this medal as a sign of their togetherness.

As soon as she sat on a chair beside his cot, she took hold of his hand. At that moment, Peter began having a seizure. "Please help him!" Still gripping his hand, Julia turned to the doctor.

"There isn't much we can do now."

As Julia watched him convulse, she began to cry. "Please," she said out loud. "Please don't go!"

The doctor touched her shoulder. "Dear, this man is too far gone. His skin is already turning blue, and his convulsions suggest his fever is beyond the turning point. I'm very sorry."

Julia would *not* accept that as an answer. She had waited years to meet her beloved — Peter — and she would not give up hope. *Dear God in heaven*, Julia silently prayed, *please heal my beloved. Mother Mary, pray for Peter. Please.* She leaned down close to his ear as he continued to convulse. "Peter, don't give up. Think of your family; think of us. Please. Don't leave me now."

Finally, he lay still. Julia released his hand so Sister June could check his pulse. "It's weak, but there's a pulse."

Julia's eyes filled with tears and she bit her lip to keep from crying. She covered his limp hand with her own. It was warm, but no longer hot. In fact, the blue tinge faded from his skin and pink replaced it. He was unconscious, but he was alive.

***

Peter opened his eyes and stared at the ceiling. He felt weak, but the dark heavy cloud in his head was gone. He had overheard the doctor say that he was "too far gone." But he was alive!

There was something on his hand. He slowly moved his head to see a white-veiled head on his hand. There was only one girl who would be keeping vigil at his cot.

***

Julia felt someone stroking her head. Her eyes flew open and she turned to see Peter smiling at her. Her heart leaped with joy and she felt giddy. "Oh, Peter. I can't believe you're alive and awake!"

He nodded.

"I thought you might be dead, but I didn't want to believe it." Julia's head lowered. "Ann found your journal and you had written, '*If you are reading this, I am most likely dead.*'"

"I can't...believe...I'm alive." Peter squeezed her hand. His voice was slurred and thick.

"It's a miracle, Peter."

"Your journal...saved...my life."

"I saw the bullet hole."

"That and...dog."

"Who?"

"Dog...tell...you later."

Julia nodded.

Peter dozed on and off for the rest of the afternoon. Julia stayed by his bedside offering prayers of thanksgiving that he was alive.

It was evening and some of the electric lights had been turned off. When he woke again, his speech was less slurred and labored. "You're still here?"

"I'm not going anywhere, at least until Sister orders me to go back to the dorm. She has given me the day off to be with you." Julia took his hand and moved it to the Miraculous Medal on the chain around his neck and sitting high on his chest. "This is for you."

"A medal?"

"Yes, I bought it for you."

A nurse came by with some pillows to prop Peter up.

"It's been a long time since I've sat up. I'm dizzy."

"No wonder. I read your journal. Were you really trapped in the basement bunker of a farmhouse?" In the weeks previous, she had prayed for him, but she had no idea of the danger he had been in. She squeezed his hand. "That must've been terrifying."

"I was and, yes, it was terrifying. I didn't think I would

make it out of there alive."

"But you did." She squeezed his hand.

***

The following morning, a young priest with small glasses and dressed in a cassock came by. Julia stood up.

"Good evening. I'm Father Ferguson from St. John's, Newfoundland. From what the doctor and nurses are saying, you've had a rather miraculous recovery."

Peter flushed. "I... suppose so."

"Father, do you really think it might be a miracle?" Julia leaned toward him to listen to his answer.

The priest nodded. "Miracles happen every day. When we see the beauty of a sunrise or the birth of a child, no one thinks twice. God works in marvelous ways, sometimes subtle and sometimes not-so-subtle."

Trying to comprehend what he was saying, Julia asked, "But do you think it might be a miracle that Peter recovered so quickly?"

"When, as the doctors say, he already had one foot in the grave, yes, I do." He paused. "I see you're wearing a Miraculous Medal. Are you Catholic, Major?"

"Yes, Father."

"Well, then you know that nothing is beyond the grasp of God. But don't forget about the miracle of the Eucharist, present in every tabernacle throughout the world. When we receive Jesus in Holy Communion, that is also miraculous."

Peter's voice was barely a whisper. "I...well, I haven't been to Mass regularly...well, since I attended university.

Perhaps this is a good time for you to hear my Confession."

The priest took a silk stole from his bag and draped it around his neck. Julia walked away and turned around to give them privacy. Julia began praying for Peter, for herself and for the war to be over.

A short time later, she heard the priest behind her clearing his throat. "You may join us again."

Peter was smiling widely at her. He was the most handsome man in the room.

"Father?"

"Yes, Miss?"

"I'd like you to hear my Confession too. I've only attended one or two Masses at the field hospital."

"Dear, this is war. You are not held accountable for Sunday Mass obligation. However, I will hear your Confession, if you still want."

"Yes."

They walked outside. The priest heard her Confession, and then they returned to Peter's bedside.

"Now would both of you like to receive Holy Communion?"

Peter nodded. "Very much so."

After receiving Communion, the priest bid them goodbye. He winked. "Don't forget the everyday miracles are important too."

Julia sat by Peter's cot, both of them silent for several moments. Finally, Peter lifted her hand and kissed the back of it. "Julia, I don't want to wait any longer."

"For what?"

"I want to ask you a question."

"Yes, yes, I will be your beloved!"

"That wasn't the question."

"It's not?" Certainly, he was teasing.

"Would you do me the honor of being my wife?"

Julia's mouth fell open, but no words would come out. This was the moment she had dreamed about for years and she couldn't speak.

Peter's gaze dropped. "If it's too..."

"Oh, Peter, I would be most honored! Yes, I will be your wife!"

***

The next day it felt like the tank had been removed from atop Peter's chest. The chain and medal Julia had put around his neck was still there, and he touched it as a symbol of their coming together.

He took a deep breath in and exhaled. Peter had more energy than he had had in days. A mild headache remained, but even his wounded leg felt remarkably better.

Yesterday, Julia told him about Smythe's passing, and Peter felt awful for sending his assistant to the post office that morning. He should've waited. Upon reflection, he realized that most of the documents Smythe carried were time-sensitive. If only Peter had known that the Huns were that close. Peter lowered his head and said a prayer for Smythe's soul.

"Major Winslow, it's time to get you up and walking. No time for self-pity." Sister June was a big-boned woman who would not take no for an answer.

He groaned. Peter knew she was correct, but even with his increased energy, he was weak and he had already visited the lavatory twice today.

"Sister June, can you inquire around to find out what happened to Coquette?"

"Coquette?"

"Yes, the dog who saved my life."

"Yes, of course, Major. By the way, you're quite the topic of conversation around here. More than a few people are saying you've had a miracle."

Yes, he thought, *a miracle that brought Julia and me together again. And the miracle of Reconciliation and Holy Communion.*

***

Peter was moved to the officers' convalescent ward as he began his recuperation. He swung his legs over the side of the cot and slowly stood up. The nurse walked beside him a few steps, then they turned around.

Quick movement across the ward caught Peter's attention. Then a bark. "Coquette!" Peter shouted, happy to see the dog that had saved his life as she raced through the barrack, a soldier with a thin moustache pulling her chain and trying to keep her from getting too close to Peter. "Hey, girl. You did a good job!"

The dog wagged her tail and tried to jump on Peter, but the soldier pulled back to restrain her.

"*Je crois qu'elle vous aime,*" the soldier said, a wide smile on his face. *I think she likes you.*

"*Le sentiment est réciproque,*" Peter responded. He had

saved Coquette and the dog had saved him. *Another miracle perhaps?* Peter paused. Wondering how she ended up in this area, he asked, "*Comment est-elle arrivée ici?*"

In French, the soldier informed Peter that he was a stretcher-bearer stationed at Le Tréport and had heard about a dog saving an Allied officer's life. Since he had a special affection for animals, the French soldier began to visit the dog every day at a fenced-in area near the British-run hospital. He had asked if he could take the dog home and for them to let him know if any of the Canadian officers had asked about a dog. He explained that he only found out that morning that Peter was there at the hospital in Le Tréport and was recuperating in the officers' ward.

***

Julia bounced into Peter's new quarters, her steps light and airy. Since August 8th, the Allies had won battle after battle, successfully pushing back the front nearly to the Belgium border. It was the end of September, but the press had reported that the Huns were admitting defeat and German troops were already surrendering in large number. Julia had been especially thankful to Sister June for allowing her to remain and take care of Peter for one day, and also for tolerating Julia's frequent visits.

She watched as Peter bent over to pet a dog that was wagging its tail and trying to lick his hand. A young French soldier with a thin mustache was pulling back on the dog's leash.

"Should I be jealous, Peter?" Julia smiled and leaned down to pet the black-and-white dog who looked to be part retriever.

"Not at all. She saved my life."

"Ah."

"Coquette went to get help for me when I was shot. So she truly did save my life. That and your journal."

Julia's eyes widened. "Well, then..." She crouched down and patted the dog. "Well done, Coquette."

"This soldier's family lives nearby. He offered to take care of Coquette, and his children have grown quite attached."

To the soldier, Peter said, "*Prends bien soin d'elle. Elle m' sauvé la vie.*" *Take good care of her. She saved my life.*

"*Oui, Monsieur.*"

As Peter took time to say goodbye to Coquette, Sister June asked Julia for assistance.

"Of course."

Julia helped Sister June stock cabinets in the barrack. "Miss Murphy, you'll be going back to the Soissons Field Hospital for the next month to help there. And if the war ends soon, you'll be staying to help close down the field hospital."

"I see."

"Don't worry. Your fellow will be fine. We'll take good care of him. He will be here for at least another month, perhaps two. His leg wound has been giving him trouble."

Before Julia could respond, the barrack door opened and Ella came in. The two embraced.

"Julia! How lovely to see you! Ann told me you were here. And that you are engaged! How splendid for you!"

"Ann tells me you have news of your own?"

"Yes, I do. But I don't think the story is over yet. I'll tell you what I can when you are free. It really does seem like the war has turned in favor of the Allies."

"Yes."

"Well, I must get some supplies, but I should be here in Le Tréport for at least a few weeks."

"It looks like I'm going back to Soissons for a short while. So we won't be able to see much of each other. Perhaps when the war is actually over?"

"Oh, yes, of course."

Julia watched Ella go to the supply closet, take out sheets, blankets and bandages, then leave.

Sigh. Julia didn't look forward to sharing the news of her transfer with Peter. But in one sense, Julia was happy to be returning to Soissons. She needed to visit the pawn shop. Her parents had sent her money, and she planned to use some of that to buy back her beloved's pocket watch. If Monsieur had already sold it, Julia would understand.

When she finished her duties assisting Sister June, she returned to Peter, who was now back on his cot and eating a light lunch of soup and croissants.

Julia sat beside his cot, staring at her hands folded on her lap.

"Is something wrong, love?"

"Nothing's wrong. I'm being transferred to Soissons for at least a month, and then possibly I'll help to close it down when the war officially ends."

"When will you have to leave?"

"Tomorrow."

"Oh." Peter lowered his head, then took hold of her

hand. Gazing into her eyes, he seemed to force a smile. "We've been through much worse, my dear, than separation. A month is a short time if we consider that we'll be together for the rest of our lives."

"I know." She squeezed his hand. "But I've become quite accustomed to being with you. I don't want to leave, but until the war ends, I am still under the command of the Red Cross."

He kissed her hand, continuing to hold onto it. "I love you and I will miss you."

"I love you, Peter, and will miss you dreadfully. I need to pack but will visit later this evening to say goodbye."

Julia stood up and Peter released her hand. Her eyes had already become moist. *I'd better leave before I start to bawl.* "See you this evening."

Chapter 22
Back in Soissons

The first item on Julia's agenda when she had a free day near Soissons was to visit Monsieur Boulanger at the pawn shop and to buy back the precious watch for her beloved. Walking down the streets of Soissons, Julia's hope soared when she saw that reconstruction had already begun.

The pawn shop's windows had been replaced, and other shops and homes on the street were in the process of rebuilding.

"Mam'selle! How are you doing?" The small man with the little glasses, a big heart and wide smile greeted her.

"I'm very well, indeed, Monsieur. And I have returned to buy back the pocket watch."

At the words, pocket watch, Monsieur's head lowered. "Oh, I am sorry. I had to sell it, *chérie*."

Julia pursed her lips and nodded. "No, no, that's quite all right, Monsieur. Please don't feel badly. I understand completely." She understood, but she was disappointed.

The man's eyes sparkled, and he let out a hearty laugh. "I tease you, *ma chérie*. I do have it here just for you."

"You do? Thank you so much! And please don't scare me so!"

"Sorry, *chérie*. Here it is."

Julia bought back the watch and put it in her coat pocket. She bid goodbye to Monsieur Boulanger and headed to Thérèse's place. She hadn't seen her at all at the field hospital since she had returned.

Her friend's street was like the others in Soissons. Houses and businesses were starting to rebuild, even though the war hadn't yet officially ended. However, the front was now 40 miles away and Julia was thankful that the wonderful citizens of this city would finally experience peace.

Looking ahead, Julia was pleased to see that the roof on Thérèse's house had been repaired. She knocked and Thérèse's mother immediately answered the door. "Julia, how marvelous to see you. Come right in."

Julia stepped inside and was astonished at the transformation the home had gone through since she was here a few months ago. Rubble had been removed. There was a parlor to the right and some of the walls had been rebuilt. The only objects scattered on the floor were a few toys.

"Julia!" Thérèse called from the end of the hall. She rushed to Julia and embraced her.

Pulling away, Julia asked, "How is Sophie?"

"See for yourself." Thérèse grabbed the banister and called up the stairs, "Sophie? Come here, please."

Two little dark-haired girls raced down the stairs. Julia could not tell which girl was Sophie and which girl was Sylvie until the first girl down the steps spoke. "Yes, Mum?"

"This is Miss Julia. Remember? She is one of the girls we've been praying for, the people who helped Mum raise money to take you to Paris to get your broken arm set and put in a cast."

The little girl's eyes widened, her mouth opened, and she smiled from ear to ear. Sophie hugged Julia, who crouched down to envelop the little girl in her arms.

"Thank you so much, Miss Julia!"

"It wasn't just me, Sophie. Many people helped."

"Well, please thank them all for me, Miss Julia! My arm is so much better. I just got the cast off two weeks ago."

"You did?"

"Uh-huh." The little girl held up her arm and turned and twisted it. Then, she and her sister ran off towards the kitchen.

"Can you stay for a cup of tea?"

"No, I'm sorry, I can't. I just wanted to drop by and see how Sophie was doing. I'm so glad she's better."

Thérèse's expression turned serious. "Julia, I don't think I shall ever be able to repay you and the others for your generosity."

"No need, Thérèse. After what you and your family have endured, we were all happy to help."

Julia turned to leave, then realized that she had forgotten to tell Thérèse her most important news.

"By the way, do you remember Major Winslow, Thérèse?"

"Of course, I do. Weren't you writing to him?"

"Yes. We are now engaged!"

"Engaged? Do tell! That's wonderful!"

Julia shared the story of the letters, the gifts and finally seeing Peter at the Le Tréport hospital.

"My goodness, what a beautiful story."

"It is, isn't it? Well, I should go."

"Goodbye, Julia."

"Goodbye, Thérèse. I will write to you when I return home to the States. Please do keep in touch."

"I will."

"Goodbye," she called to Thérèse's mum at the end of the hall.

Back at her dorm in the *château* at the field hospital, Julia found Charlotte. The lack of new casualties and the passing of other soldiers had made the death ward obsolete, but her friend seemed distracted and not inclined to chat.

"Is everything all right, Charlotte?"

"Yes, I suppose it is. Please don't worry about me. I'm so happy that you and Major Winslow — your beloved — will be getting married."

***

Julia had hoped that the month of October would race by, especially since she had followed the news of the impending negotiations between the Allies and the Axis nations. But October had gone by painfully slow, and she found herself missing Peter more and more each day. Each time she read his early sonnets, she fell more in love with him. Julia lived for his letters and sonnets, but they became rather poor substitutes for his presence.

Peter had suffered a setback with his leg and another operation was necessary, but his last letter gave the impression he was doing much better.

***

November 2, 1918

Peter spent most of his days reading the newspaper or writing letters to family back home and, of course, to Julia. His wretched leg wound was better now that he had undergone additional surgery. But he missed Julia. Since she had left for Soissons, Peter felt like half of him was missing.

Reading the most recent news of the negotiations, Peter suspected that the war would be over within a week or two, hopefully by mid-November, which meant that Julia would return soon after that.

Other convalescing officers greeted daily visitors. Since they were at the end of the war, protocol became less stringent and many of the British and French soldiers welcomed guests each day.

Perhaps he should concentrate on writing another sonnet for Julia. Out of the corner of his eye, he saw someone pick up a chair and move closer to him. Lifting his head, he drew in a breath, then smiled. She was there, right in front of him! "Julia!"

"Peter!"

They embraced, kissed and embraced again. Now that she was here, Peter didn't want to let her go. She finally pulled away and sat down on the edge of his cot.

"You're here for good, my dear?"

"No, just for a leave. Only two days. I guess Sister Betty couldn't stand my moping around, so she encouraged me to visit you. Then we'll hopefully only have a few weeks before I'm back permanently."

"Well, we must enjoy our time while we are together."

"Yes, we should."

They kissed and Peter felt whole again.

Chapter 23
Home for Christmas

After two days of visiting with Peter, Julia returned to Soissons. On November 11th, Armistice Day, Julia received orders that indicated she would travel to Le Tréport on November 19th. She remained there in service to the Red Cross until Peter was discharged on December 4th. Ann left the week after Armistice Day and was reunited with her beau Theo back in the States. Charlotte and Ella shared exciting news of their own on the romance front.

Peter was now ambulatory and required only a cane.

Before they set out for Paris, Julia and Peter took the *funiculaire* train through the cliff and down to the beach at Le Tréport. They walked along the shore, hand in hand, admiring the tiny pebbles mixed with sand and waves rolling onto the beach. They sat on a large rock near the water.

"I can't believe I'm finally going home." Peter sighed, his breath visible in the cold December air. "And taking with me my beautiful fiancée."

"I'm looking forward to meeting your family, Peter."

"I hope your parents aren't too put off by the Canadian who asked their daughter to marry him."

"I promise they won't be."

"Well, I promise that my family will love you as much as I do. I love you, Julia, and I look forward to spending the rest of my life with you."

Julia had read those words in the journal many times,

but she would never tire of hearing him say them out loud. "I love you, Peter. I just can't believe..."

"What?"

"I can't believe we're here, together, on this breathtaking — and very cold — beach." She laughed. "And that you and I will be married."

The waves lapped against the beach and the crisp cool sea air made Julia shiver. She rubbed her hands together. "I should have worn gloves and a hat, I suppose."

Peter took gloves from his jacket and held them out to her. As she put on the oversized gloves, he took his scarf from around his neck and wrapped it around her head and under her chin. With his hands on either side of her face, Peter leaned down and gently kissed Julia on the lips.

***

A few days later, the couple traveled by train to Paris. They visited the Eiffel Tower and even took the elevator to the top level. It was thrilling and exciting for Julia to be on the arm of her beloved and looking out at the Parisian skyline. From that high point, Julia could also see the destruction Paris had endured during the Great War.

Despite the hat, gloves and warm wool coat, Julia shivered, and Peter pulled her to an embrace.

The next stop was *Le Louvre*, then an early dinner at a restaurant on the *Champs Élysées*. The last place they would visit before sundown would be Peter's brother's grave.

***

At John's grave, Peter made the sign of the cross and bowed his head. Out of the corner of his eye, he saw that

Julia did the same. While he said his prayer silently, she recited a Hail Mary out loud and Peter joined in. "Now and at the hour of our death. Amen." Never before had he been so close to death and never before had he been so filled with gratitude that he was alive. He took hold of Julia's hand and kissed it.

***

The following day was the Feast of the Immaculate Conception and the couple took the street car to Notre Dame Cathedral to attend Mass. As Julia knelt in the pew, she thanked God and Our Lady for her beloved — for Peter — and for their 'great love' borne out of a 'great war.' She gazed up at the crucifix. Jesus suffered greatly because He loved us. His was — and is — a 'great love' borne out of great suffering.

***

They set sail for America on December 9th, arriving at the harbor in New York City on December 16th. Julia was excited beyond measure that her entire family showed up to greet them. She had already sent her mother a telegram, informing her that she would be bringing home her fiancé, a Canadian officer named Peter. Hugs were shared and introductions made, and the group took the train back to Philadelphia. Jack kept pestering Peter with questions about the army. Jimmy and Joey asked endless questions about Canada. But Peter didn't seem to mind.

After a two-day visit with the Murphy family, Julia and Peter took the train first to Ottawa, the capital of Canada, then to Arnprior and to the Winslow family home. Julia was overwhelmed by Peter's family's kindness and affection. Peter had already written to his family about his injuries, but when Mrs. Winslow saw that he was using a cane, she expressed concern about her son's health. Peter assured her that he was on the mend and would recover fully.

Maggie asked rapid-fire questions of Julia for the first hour or so. "Was it love at first sight?"

"It's very difficult to experience love at first sight in the midst of a gruesome field hospital. That wasn't very romantic."

"You're correct about that, love." Peter squeezed her hand.

Maggie kept the questions coming: "How did you meet? "How did you know you loved Peter?"

Julia reflected for a moment. Should she tell the girl that she had bought gifts for her beloved years before she even knew him? And that before she knew he was her beloved, he wound up with most of the gifts anyway? And that perhaps two of those gifts saved his life, the journal slowing down the bullet, and the medal when he was ill with the flu? Or that Peter was one of the most eloquent sonnet authors? Perhaps another time. Today it was best to tell it more simply.

"First, we saw each other occasionally at the hospital. When your brother was transferred, we ended up becoming cordial correspondents. And then? Well, then I discovered that your brother writes the most beautiful sonnets." Julia paused for effect. "And that's when I knew he was my beloved."

Maggie let out a sigh. "How romantic."

After a dinner of tourtière, Shepherd's Pie, salad and apple crumble for dessert, Peter took Julia for a stroll to see the park and town hall. They walked slowly because

Peter continued to use a cane. A misty snow fell, and although they could see their breaths, it wasn't as cold up in Canada as Julia thought it would be.

Their trip ended all too quickly, with Julia returning to Philadelphia to spend the week before Christmas with her family and to begin planning their spring wedding. Peter would join her on Christmas Eve, after he spent time with his family in Arnprior.

***

After Midnight Mass on Christmas, Julia could hardly wait to tell Peter the whole story about the gifts and to give him the final gift: the pocket watch.

When they arrived back at her family's house, all was quiet. Traditionally, the Murphy family opened gifts Christmas morning, then attended Mass at noon.

Across the living room, the balsam tree's glass balls shimmered against the dimmed gas lights her mother had left on. After taking off his coat, Peter helped Julia take off hers then hung them in the closet. She removed her boots and rushed to the Christmas tree to find her gift to Peter.

"You seem very anxious, my dear."

"Oh, I am." She turned and held out the small package. "Merry Christmas, Peter."

Opening it, he took the watch out and held it in front of them. "My goodness, this is beautiful. And just what I need." Peter turned the watch over and stared at the engraving. He pinched his lips as if he didn't want to say something.

"Don't you like it?"

"Of course, I like it. I will treasure it always. But..."

"But?"

"The engraver put in the wrong year. It says '*Merry Christmas to my Beloved, December, 1917.*'"

"It's not wrong at all. I bought it before we met. In fact, you've now received *all* the gifts I've bought or made for you."

"I have?" His eyebrows rose. "You mean the socks?"

Julia nodded. "Yes. Remember you picked them up from the donation bin. Before you began writing to me."

"The wool socks were made specifically for *me*?"

"Well, it was before I knew that you were my beloved."

"Ah, yes." He laughed. "Now, I understand. And the other gifts?"

"The journal that Charlotte gave you."

"You bought the journal for *me*?"

"Again, it was before I knew you were my future husband. And this pocket watch, and the Miraculous Medal."

"Wait a minute. You knit the socks, bought the journal, the watch and the medal for *me*, but *before* you knew me. Do I have that right?"

"Yes, that's correct. I began buying gifts for you when I was 17.

"I've never heard of such a thing."

"Well, it was my way of trying to be patient about meeting my beloved. And, yes, I know it's rather...odd."

"Not at all. It's quite endearing." He caressed her cheek. "It makes me love you more that you bought gifts for me before you knew me. Now, may I give you *your* Christmas gifts?"

"Yes!"

From behind his back, Peter pulled out what looked to be a parchment held together with…was that a ring? Yes! It was a gold ring with a small diamond in the center and miniature sapphires on either side. "Oh, Peter! It's beautiful!"

Peter took the ring off and placed it on Julia's finger. "Merry Christmas, love. This is the ring that will make our upcoming nuptials official."

"It's lovely."

"It's actually *Grand-mere's* ring."

"So it's an heirloom?"

"Indeed it is. And don't forget to read what's on the parchment paper."

"Oh, yes!" Unrolling the parchment, Julia found that it was another sonnet. "It's wonderful!"

"You haven't read it yet."

"I know I will treasure this, as I do the other sonnets."

"I hope you like it as much as the others."

She read out loud, her heart and voice full of emotion.

Ellen Gable

Still Lost, If Not For Stars

'Tis one soul's plight to cut through ice and snow.
Another's journey o'er hot desert sand.
Yet all proceed, their will set to demand
Arrival at the place their heart needs go.

Still lost, if not for stars to glow and guide,
Forlorn, if not emboldened through night,
The traveler in the dark seeks angels' light;
As shepherds sought their song at Christmastide.

So as the Holy Child descends to all,
And as the Magi humbly came to stall,
I come to you, beloved, bearing gifts:
Of honour and of service, fit for queen,
And consolation for the wounds you've seen,
And love as long as snow and sand are drift.

Epilogue
One Year Later

December 20, 1919

Julia stared at the Lit Brothers Christmas display glowing with electric lights. Just two years ago, she had stood in this same spot trying to decide what to buy for her beloved. So much had happened in two short years. She grew from a naïve and carefree — almost foolish — girl to a mature woman who had experienced things no one should ever have to experience. But she had also grown into a woman who was blessed to experience great love.

The past year since the war had ended had been challenging — and busy. Peter had gotten employment in Ottawa as a translator, so Julia had stayed in Philadelphia to plan their wedding. Four months they had remained apart, and Julia had counted the days until their nuptials.

Their wedding was a small affair in Philadelphia with close family and friends. They honeymooned in Niagara Falls (on the Canadian side) for a few days, then spent the next week fixing up their new home in Arnprior.

The past eight months of marriage had also been one of adjustments. For Julia, she had to become accustomed to living in another country. Canada was similar to the United States in many respects, and the people overall seemed very courteous and, of course, it was colder in the Ottawa Valley than in Philadelphia.

Despite the challenges, they were both ecstatic to be expecting a child in late spring.

They had traveled by train to Philadelphia to visit her parents and brothers for five days before Christmas. They planned to return to Canada on Boxing Day. They hoped to visit Ann and Theo at some point before leaving for Canada. Ann and her husband recently bought a farmhouse in a town in South Jersey called Runnemede.

The display window was filled with colorful Christmas plates, vases and ornaments. Snow had begun to fall as she contemplated going inside the store. Before she could decide, however, she heard Peter's soft voice behind her.

"Ready, love?"

"Yes," she said, turning toward her husband. The two made their way to the trolley across the street.

Charlotte's Honor

Great War Great Love: Book Two

is scheduled to be released in late 2018

Acknowledgments

Julia's Gifts has been a labor of love that I have been working on for four years. Most of that time has been spent in research, finding out more about the last year of the Great War than I ever expected to know.

Special thanks to the Arnprior and District Museum (Cathy Rodger) for lending us the vintage clothes to photograph the cover. Thank you also to Sydney Faour for posing for the cover.

Thank you to Cheryl Thompson for the excellent job of copyediting. Special thanks to Theresa Linden, who went above and beyond the role of proofreader. Special thanks also to Christopher Blunt for valuable editing suggestions. To Nick Lauer, Ann Frailey, Sarah Loten and Carolyn Astfalk for proofreading and helpful editing advice.

My gratitude to Ian Frailey for coming up with the series title: *Great War Great Love*.

It's extremely helpful when an author happens to have a dear friend who is also bilingual. Thank you, Ginger Regan, for making sure the French spoken by the characters was correct and all the accents were in the right place.

It's hard to convey my gratitude to my incredibly talented husband, James, in a few short sentences. This book truly would not exist without his assistance. Special thanks for listening patiently as I shared plot lines and character studies and received valuable feedback. I am also indebted to my husband for composing the beautiful and moving sonnets included in this book.

About the Author

Ellen Gable (Hrkach) is an award-winning author (2010 IPPY Gold, 2015 IAN finalist), publisher (2016 CALA), editor, Marketing Director for *Live the Fast*, self-publishing book coach, speaker, NFP teacher, Marriage Preparation Instructor and past president of the Catholic Writers Guild. She is an author of eight books and a contributor to numerous others. Her books have been collectively downloaded over 600,000 times on Kindle. She and her husband, James, are the parents of five adult sons and seven precious souls in heaven. In her spare time, Ellen enjoys reading on her Kindle, researching her family tree, and watching classic movies and TV shows. Her website is located at www.ellengable.com.

Ellen enjoys hearing from her readers: please
email her at fullquiverpublishing@gmail.com

Published by
Full Quiver Publishing
PO Box 244
Pakenham ON K0A2X0
Canada
www.fullquiverpublishing.com

Made in the USA
Columbia, SC
16 November 2017